The Kittens

by Allison Angel

Dripping with Anticipation

I ran up to my room that afternoon still wearing the white top and plaid skirt I'd worn to school. It was one of my favorite skirts because it showed off my legs up to mid-thigh. My legs are long and thin and I once overheard my friend's dad refer to them as "coltish", whatever that means. I had my hair was in a blonde ponytail that swung as I ran. The house was quiet and I didn't expect my mom home from work for a couple hours. This was my chance. In my room filled with stuffed animals and cheerleading trophies and posters from my favorite bands, I got down on my knees and lifted up the pink ruffle on my bed. I reached under my bed and pulled out a big box.

I was so excited that my hands trembled. I'd ordered it all online and today was the big day. I opened the box and carefully laid each piece on my bed. It had to be perfect. I looked down at the outfit and bit my lip, nervous and excited. I'd never worn anything like this. Anyone who knew me would be shocked if they saw me wearing this. Sweet little Bree? The adorable blonde cheerleader? No way!

The dress was a tiny black backless mini-dress that was advertised as a 'wet look halter mini-dress'. The thin material was shiny metallic and it plunged low in the front and was so short that it would barely cover my cute little butt. I blushed just looking at it.

I also had fishnet thigh-highs and 6" sky-high clear platform heels that I found on a website for strippers. The shoes had clear platform heels with a sexy six-inch stiletto heel that the packages said "makes any occasion into a sultry one". How could a boy resist?

Finally, I had a black velvet ribbon choker for my neck and a white thong with "Princess" spelled out on the front in silvery rhinestones. I smiled to myself when I saw the little thong. I picked it up and touched the little rhinestones. Tonight, for the first time, a boy would take my panties off.

Tonight I was losing my virginity.

Pretty Little Virgin

I took a shower and shaved myself completely down there. I was already so wet – shaving myself just got me hotter. I couldn't wait to feel Jake's cock penetrate me, taking my cherry. I moaned in the shower and closed my eyes as the water hit my smooth bare pussy. I knew waiting was the right thing to do, but I'd been dying to have sex since I was about fourteen. I couldn't help thinking I had a stronger sex drive than most girls. I just couldn't stop fantasizing about men taking me. And I'd waited this long – until my senior year! – because my family and my church had made it clear that good girls wait until marriage. But I couldn't wait any longer.

I dried off my glistening body and rubbed lotion all over, feeling my smooth taut skin and making me squirm with excitement. I stepped into the little thong and felt it slide up between my firm cheeks. I'd never worn a thong before – my mother would never allow it. I felt so sexual, so hot, and so exotic. I looked down at the little rhinestone letters on the thong: "Princess". I felt like a princess! I turned around in the mirror and looked at my bare bottom. For years boys – and men -- had watched my ass in my skirts. Now one of them was finally getting his hands on it.

I did my makeup just wearing the thong. I saw myself in the mirror. My eyes were dark and smoky and my lips were wet with pink cherry lip gloss. I put matching hot pink nail polish on my toes and fingers. I wore my hair up but with blonde strands hanging down like I'd seen in some photos of a porn star on the internet. I put the choker tight around my neck.

Back in my room, I pulled on my dress. It was skin-tight and clung to every curve. Because it was backless and very low-cut in the front, I couldn't wear a bra. My breasts stood out defiantly and my hard little nipples poked through the thin material. My breasts weren't the biggest but they look big because I'm so skinny; I'd always been proud of how perky they are. I smiled at the little slut looking back at me in the mirror.

I slid the thigh-highs up my long thin legs. I loved the way they felt and the way the fishnet pattern made me look like a naughty girl. There was a gap between the top of my thigh-highs and the hem of my tiny dress that revealed my bare thighs. I was so proud of my thigh gap – all the other cheerleaders were so jealous. I liked showing it off. I strapped on the 6" stripper heels and felt so tall. I was only 5'6 and 110 pounds but in the heels I looked like a towering runway model. The heels really made my legs look long. And my little ass stuck out adorably in the dress. I knew if I bent over at all, my cheeks would peek out.

I smiled in the mirror and giggled. "Oh, excuse me, sir, did I drop my napkin?" I bent over, my ass in the air. The dress slid up to reveal my bare cheeks. I felt so wild. So naughty. So sexy.

I slid my hands up my dress, feeling the silky panties over my freshly shaven mound. I imagined his hands there, touching me, then his fingers finding the thong strap and slowly pulling them down, exposing my untouched body. I bit my lip, pulling my thong down my thighs to my knees. My finger found my wet pussy. I was so ready.

I looked at the clock and saw it was 5:00 already. I had to hurry! I pulled my thong back up and adjusted my dress. My mom would be home in a

half-hour and if she saw me like this I'd be grounded

for life!

Car Trouble

I snuck out to my car and drove off. Jake was totally worth all of this effort. We'd been dating for years. We were the "it couple" in our high school. But he swore he was the only virgin left in the senior class, and he was probably right, except for the guys who are going to end up serial killers. The girls in our school had a hard-earned reputation for serious sluttery. Jake was good-looking and the captain of the cross-country team, and if he wasn't dating me, I'm sure he would have lost his virginity years ago. But he waited for me. Reluctantly, but he waited.

For years, he'd tried to get me in bed. We'd make out for hours. I could feel all the tension in his body dying for release. And his hands exploring my body made me a little sex kitten in heat. But I'd listened to my parents and my pastor. I waited. And so did Jake. And tonight I would surprise him. It was his birthday and I told him I wanted to have a little surprise party alone with him, so he borrowed the keys to his older sister's apartment while she was out of town.

I peeked out the window from our kitchen to see if any neighbors were outside. It looked like the coast was clear; I only had to cover twenty feet between our kitchen door and my car. I walked out, suddenly feeling so wild out in public in this outfit. I climbed into the car hurriedly, my dress sliding up as I sat down.

In the car, I turned up the radio and thought about how it would go. As soon as he saw me, he would know he was getting lucky. I usually dressed conservatively, except on game days when we wore our cheerleading uniforms to school. My dad never really liked our uniforms – the skirts were too skimpy, the tops were too tight and showed off our bare midriffs. And, of course, whenever his little daughter was thrown in the air, the whole world could see my panties peeking out. So when Jake saw me dressed like this, he'd know instantly that he was getting some. I was sure of it.

I imagined myself like I'd seen in the porn I watched on the internet. I would drop down on my knees first and suck his cock. I was ready for that – I practiced on a cucumber that was even bigger than Jake's cock. I'd seen his before, and often felt it under his pants, desperate to get to me. It wasn't very big, at least not compared to the men in the internet porn videos. I imagined Jake would take me to the bed and we'd make love missionary-style, because it's the most traditional and romantic.

But I hoped I'd end up like the girl in the porn video: face down with my ass in the air while he mounted me from behind and held my head down by my hair.

Oh, it got me so hot to watch that girl get pounded. I was thinking about the way the man forced his cock into her pussy, deep and hard, while she moaned. I was getting so wet. I couldn't wait to feel Jake inside me.

Suddenly the car made a strange noise and the engine had no power when I pressed the gas. I stomped on the gas but nothing happened. I couldn't believe it. It was an old piece-of-crap car; I wished I were one of those private school girls in their brand-new BMWs. I pulled over as far as I could get to the side of the road before it finally died. Great. I didn't know anything about cars, but my dad was always telling me to do stuff like check the oil or something. I never did. He always ended up taking care of it for me anyway. Now I was screwed. I'd have to call Jake to come get me – I couldn't call anyone else, dressed like this.

I reached for my bag on the passenger seat. It wasn't there! No phone! No anything! In my hurry to leave the house, I'd forgotten my bag. I was stranded on the side of the road. And it was getting dark.

Biker Trouble

I pulled the little handle that popped the hood. I didn't want to get out of the car dressed like this, but I didn't even bring a jacket or anything to cover up. Now I didn't have a choice; the world was going to see me in this slutty dress. So I stepped out of the car nervously. There wasn't much of a shoulder on the road so the car was almost blocking the road. There was nowhere for me to hide. Luckily there wasn't a lot of traffic on this road. I walked up to the front of the car, teetering in my heels, and opened the hood. Nothing looked broken. I had no idea what I was looking at.

I heard a car driving up from behind. When it got even with me, I heard the driver blow his horn. A guy leaned out the passenger side and yelled, "Hey, baby, want a ride?" and leered at me in my slutty dress. I covered my perky breasts with my hands, well aware that without a bra my breasts stood out like I was offering them.

I was getting scared. I didn't want to walk, alone, along a dark road. But I couldn't just sit here. What should I do? I bit my lip nervously.

Suddenly I heard the roar of a motorcycle coming from the other direction. The man on the bike watched me as he drove by, and then he slowed down, turned around, and came up behind my car and stopped. He leaned his bike to the side, kicked out the kickstand with a big boot, and got off his bike. He took off his helmet and I saw he was an older man, big and rough looking, in jeans and black boots and a leather jacket. He had a few days stubble. He was good-looking in a rough kind of way, if you liked the kind of men who worked with their hands. He did not look like a gentleman.

I felt my young body trembling as I heard his heavy boots crunching as he walked up to the front of my car. He stopped and his eyes went up and down my body, taking in every curve. I blushed. I was used to men checking me out, but usually they just snuck a peek at me. He was looking me over openly, like I was a piece of meat and he was a hungry dog. For some reason, probably because I'd been so turned on all day thinking about losing my virginity to Jake, his eyes on my body got me wet all over again.

"Hey, babydoll, car trouble?" he said, openly staring at my young body. I crossed my arms over my chest, but I couldn't hide everything. I saw his eyes move down to my bare thighs.

"Yes, umm, can I borrow your phone to call my dad? He's a cop and he'll be here any minute." Of course, my dad wasn't a cop. He was the church's accountant. He'd certainly have no chance if this big biker wanted his daughter.

The biker smiled, "Pretty girl like you out here all alone without your phone?"

I nodded my cute little blonde head. I felt so exposed. I was almost naked in front of a stranger and he was clearly enjoying the view.

"Well, I don't have my phone, either," he said, shaking his head as he looked me over.

I didn't believe him. I was breathing hard, so scared.

"But I can take a look at your engine for you, gorgeous."

I breathed a sigh of relief. "Oh, thank you! Do you know how to fix cars?" I smiled innocently.

He shrugged. "Let's take a look." He leaned over the engine and touched some parts. I leaned over too, but I tugged my dress down in the back so my little bare bottom wasn't exposed.

He stood up and wiped his hands on his jeans, staring at my ass. "Nothing we can do here. Gotta get it to a shop."

"Oh no!" I cried. I was really stuck. It was getting darker, long shadows stretching across the road as the sun sank in the sky. I was alone on the side of the road with a dirty biker. I imagined they'd find my body in a ditch.

Going for a Ride

The biker looked at me, "I'll tell you what – I'll give you a ride to a phone, OK?"

I stood there trembling. I didn't know what to do. I'd never ridden on a motorcycle before. I certainly never went anywhere with a stranger. And he seemed dangerous and dirty. But what choice did I have? I couldn't stay here alone, in the dark.

"I, umm, OK, thanks?" I looked up, confused and scared, my whole body trembling.

A smile spread across his face. I walked with him to his big motorcycle, struggling on the gravel in my high heels.

"Here, let me help," he grabbed my arm, wrapping his thick muscular hand around my skinny arm. He guided me to his motorcycle. He picked me up by my hips without asking and placed me on the back of the bike, side-saddle, and smiled, "Straddle the bike, baby." He watched as I blushed and then obeyed, lifting my long leg over and straddling the bike. My little dress slid up – there was nothing I could do about it – and he smiled broadly when he saw my little thong peeking out.

"Princess, huh?" he smiled, looking right between my legs. I blushed and put my hands between my legs, but he was enjoying my long legs spread open in the fishnet thigh-highs. He climbed on the bike in front of me, right between my legs. He reached back and grabbed my legs, squeezing them tight around his waist. He patted my thigh. "You're going to need to hold on tight, babydoll." I couldn't believe it; a grown man touching my thighs like that. It was so wrong.

The motorcycle roared to life between my legs. I only had a tiny thong between the motorcycle and my pussy, and I was already dripping wet. Feeling the vibration just made me hotter. I wrapped my arms around him. He was well-built and strong. The motorcycle pulled away, sending rocks flying on the shoulder toward my stranded car. I wrapped my arms around him tighter, not daring to let go.

As he drove, my little dress climbed way up my thighs in the wind. I didn't dare reach down to fix it. If we drove by anyone, they'd see a grown man with a little half-naked sex-kitten on the back of his bike. I felt him reach back with one hand and feel my leg, sliding up my thigh. I yelled "Stop!" in the wind but he couldn't hear me – or he ignored me. His hand found my thigh, and then up to my little ass. He was groping me while driving the motorcycle, knowing I'd be too terrified to let go long enough to push his hand away.

I couldn't help getting turned on. I was scared, but it was so exciting. I was riding a motorcycle with a biker who looked old enough to be my dad, and he was feeling me up. The rumble of the motorcycle between my legs was making my little virgin pussy dripping-wet with excitement. I forgot myself for a moment, feeling the wind in my hair and the man groping me and imagined I was little slutty biker girl out with her man.

He pulled into a gravel parking lot in front of a rough-looking bar. He parked the bike next to a line of other motorcycles and turned it off. He turned in his seat, still between my smooth young thighs, and smiled mockingly at me. "Did you like the ride, baby?"

No Free Rides

I blushed, but I nodded my cute little blonde head. A little smile played on my lips. "Yeah, the ride was OK, but you groped me!" I pouted and pushed his hand away from my thigh. He'd never let go.

He laughed. "Come on, baby, you know the rules: no free rides. Gas, grass, or ass, right?"

I blushed but I couldn't help smiling a little. Our eyes met. He had the coolest slate-gray eyes. Maybe he wasn't so bad after all. He climbed off and picked me up by my hips again, without waiting for permission. He lifted me off the bike so easily. He was so strong, so powerful. I felt a chill down my back while he took control of my body. When I was on the ground, he kept his hands on my young hips while I tugged my dress down. He shook his head sadly while I covered my little bare bottom.

He smiled down at me and winked, "Ready, Princess?"

I nodded my cute little blonde head, feeling his hands firmly on my young hips. This was so scary – I was glad it was almost over. I just needed to call Jake and escape. I knew good, safe, reliable preppy Jake would get here as fast as he could to rescue me from this wolf. But the way he looked at me gave me a thrill. It felt so dangerous to be alone with him, and I could still feel the vibration of his motorcycle between my virgin thighs.

It was already dark outside the biker bar and he led me to the door with his hand possessively on my smooth bare back just above my ass. There was a man in the shadows peeing against the wall unsteadily. He looked back over his shoulder and I could see his drunken eyes in the green light from the neon sign that read, 'Bikers welcome'. He leered at me, "Damn, that bitch is hot."

I blushed, but I liked the attention. I'd always been the good girl – hard-working straight-A student, head cheerleader, honor society, debate club, church youth group, student council vice president (under Jake, our president). But tonight I felt like a very bad girl. I was going into a bar – I'd never been in a bar before! And not just any bar: a dirty biker bar. And I was going in with a rough-looking older man who couldn't take his eyes off my body. He obviously had very bad intentions. Why did his bad intentions make me feel so... good?

Buy Me a Drink?

Inside it was loud and crowded, but it felt like the music suddenly stopped and time froze when we walked in. Every man in the bar turned and looked at me. In the light, I realized just how slutty I looked. My breasts stood out, so firm and young and fresh, and my nipples were so hard through the thin dress. With the choker around my neck and my dark eye makeup, I was sure I looked like a stripper. I instinctively moved closer to the biker – my biker – because I felt like all these men would tear me to pieces. I felt his arm around me, finding my hip and pulling me close. He led me up to the bar.

I looked up at him, suddenly very scared and feeling so naked and exposed before all these strange men. I didn't dare look any of them in the eyes. The biker kept his hand on my hip. "Please, where is the phone?" I begged.

He smiled down at me darkly, "It's in the back," he nodded his head past the pool table. I'd have to walk through a crowd of bikers. "Do you have a quarter hidden somewhere in that dress?" He looked down at my firm young body in my dress again, admiring me. I gulped, but my body reacted to his eyes, my back arching a little, sticking my breasts out. Why was I showing off for him? I had to stop this.

"Oh! No... I... I don't have a quarter. Can you lend me one?"

He smiled, "Yeah, sure, I'll give you a quarter, but you have to give me something first."

I blushed. "What?" I demanded. This had gone too far.

"Relax, baby," he smiled down at me, so sure of himself. "I just want a little kiss."

"No."

"Come on, baby, just a little kiss. Plant one right here." He pointed to his rough unshaven cheek.

I knew I shouldn't do it – he'd already had his fun feeling me up. But I knew this little fantasy would be over as soon as I made that call, and I felt like such a wild child, like one of those naughty girls at school with bad reputations. I leaned up to give him a kiss. Just as my soft pink-cherry lips got close, he turned his head so our lips met.

"Oh!" I pulled away and hit him playfully on his powerful arm.

He laughed and I couldn't help smiling.

"Now where's my quarter?" I demanded with a playful smile. I felt his hand, still on my hip. I'd gotten used to him touching me.

"No, baby," he laughed, "you have to kiss me first. I kissed you. Now it's your turn."

"Oh, fine," I pouted, pretending to be angry but feeling so flushed. I was flirting with a grown man at a biker bar while dressed like a stripper. I could never tell anyone about this night, but I knew I'd never forget it. And I was sure Jake was going to get the ride of his life – my little virgin body was ready to climb the walls.

I tilted my head up and we kissed. I even closed my eyes. I felt his tongue part my lips and enter my mouth. I was making out with a grown man in front of everyone! I was a total slut! And it made my body tremble with desire.

"Now give it to me!" I demanded, looking up at him with my big green eyes.

"Fine, babydoll. Let me get change. What are you drinking?"

"Drinking? I'm not old enough to drink," I whispered. I looked over at the bartender who was desperately trying to rip my dress off with his eyes. "Excuse me, sir? Can we have change?"

He shrugged, his eyes on my breasts. "This ain't a bank, sweetheart."

I turned back to the biker and he laughed. "I guess we do it my way, right baby?" He ordered us two shots and the bartender poured clear liquid in tiny glasses. I'd never had a shot before. I'd snuck some beer with my friends and my dad sometimes gave me a sip of his wine, but I'd never really drank alcohol before. He put a quarter on the bar and my shot glass on top of it. "Drink up, baby."

The Star of the Bar

I knew I should just take the quarter, make the call, and get out of here. I could hear my mom in my ear yelling at me about how dangerous this was. But I wasn't a little kid anymore. I could take care of myself. And I could stop this at any time. Jack would be here as soon as I called. But it was so hot. The men in the bar couldn't stop staring at me. I was the only girl in there except for an older heavyset woman with a lot of tattoos. I felt like a star. All the eyes were on me!

I looked up at the biker and picked up my shot. "Cheers!" I smiled, acting brave and feeling so mature. "Cheers!" he smiled. I drank the shot. And I almost threw up! It burned on the way down and my eyes watered immediately. "Oh!"

He laughed and handed me a beer. I swallowed some of it to wash the taste out of my mouth. "God, that's horrible!" I gagged.

"What's your name?" he smiled and leaned over the bar.

I wiped my mouth and looked up at him. "I'm Bree."

"I'm Brett." I felt his hand on my hip slide to my ass. I grabbed his hand and pulled it back to my hip.

"Hello, Brett," I smiled up at him. "You're not being a gentleman."

He smiled back and swigged his beer. "I never promised you that, baby Bree."

I picked up the quarter and turned it over in my hand. Bree and Brett. It sounded so cute, like a celebrity couple. But my little fantasy acting like a slut in public was over. I'd go make the call. I looked back past the pool table. It was dark in the back and I'd have to pass through a bunch of drunk guys.

"Want to walk me to the phone, Brett?" I smiled up at him like a little flirt.

"You're a needy little thing, aren't you?" he smiled, rubbing my hip so my dress climbed up a little more. Any higher and I'd be flashing my ass to the whole bar. "What are you going to do for me?" He tilted his beer bottle back and emptied it. He signaled to the bartender, who lined up two more shots and another beer.

I sighed, "Fine, another kiss?" Secretly I wanted him to kiss me. He was totally wrong for me. He had to be old enough to be my dad. He had dirt under his fingernails. And he was no gentleman. My mom would lock me in my room for decades if she saw me just talking to Brett! But this night would be my

secret – forever. The night I went to a dirty biker

bar and acted like a slut.

But he shook his head no. "You kiss like a virgin."

"Oh! I do not!"

"Yeah, you do. Tell you what: take a shot and kiss

me. But for real this time. Then I'll walk you back."

I reached up on the bar. I was more scared of the

shot than the kiss. But I wasn't going to let him

treat me like a little kid. I threw back the shot and

gagged, but I wiped my mouth with my hand and

slammed the glass down on the bar like the other

men at the bar did.

I turned to him and put my arms around his neck,

pressing my body against his. I pressed my soft lips

against his, kissing softly, then nibbling his lower lip,

then sucking on it. Our mouths met and we kissed,

our tongues entwined, right there at the bar with everyone watching. His hands found my ass and gripped each cheek tightly with his rough hands under my dress.

"Was that better?" I smiled up at him when we separated. He kept his hands on my bare bottom, pulling my body against his.

"It was better for me," the big guy next to us at the bar growled and a bunch of guys laughed.

A guy behind us yelled, "Yeah, that bitch is hot! Let me see that ass again!" Brett turned and gave him a look that had a clear malevolent warning in it. I belonged to Brett and anyone else who wanted me was going to have to go through him. Why did that turn me on?

A Shot Too Far

Obviously everyone had seen my bare bottom when he'd pulled my dress up. I felt so wild and naughty. They saw my thong! I was such a little slut! I was going to the phone, but I felt a little reluctant to go. I loved the attention. I loved feeling like a wild girl. But I smiled back over my shoulder, "Sorry, guys, I belong to Brett!"

I put my hand in his and we held hands as we walked back to the phone. I felt so hot. My face was flushed and I was little unsteady. I smiled up at him over my shoulder, "I'm good for your reputation!" I giggled.

He watched the way my ass moved in the little dress. "Yeah, baby, you're good for a lot of things."

The phone was in a dark corner by the bathroom. I knew why the guy was peeing outside when we came in: it smelled terrible back here. I picked up the phone and it had a dial tone. I was a little surprised: I'd never actually used a pay phone before. Turns out, you can call 'collect' so the person you're calling pays for it. I didn't even need to earn my quarter.

I dialed Jake's number while Brett felt me up. His hands slid up and down my sides while I felt him grind his hips into my little bottom. I felt something hard and hot pressing against me. I couldn't help it: I stuck my little ass out for him.

It rang and rang while Brett pulled my hips out so my ass was against his cock. He kicked my feet apart so my long legs were spread. A group of men at the pool table were watching the show. I felt so hot and wild. I was dripping wet. Then I got voicemail.

"Um, hi, Jake, it's me. My car broke down and I need you to pick me up." I put my hand over the receiver. "Brett, what is the address here?"

He shrugged, grinding on my young body. "I love this ass, baby."

"Please???" I begged.

He pointed to the phone. It was written right there: Buck's Tavern, 272 West Township Road.

"I'm at Buck's Tavern at 272 West Township Road. And you'd better hurry!" I yelped as I felt Brett's hands under my dress. He took the phone from my hand and hung it up. Brett had my dress up over my hips, showing off my little cheerleader ass for the crowd. I pulled away and tugged my dress down, but I stumbled a little in my high heels. I was lightheaded. Suddenly I felt very alone, in a biker bar, with a grown man groping me in front of everyone.

Brett smiled hungrily down at me. "Don't worry, baby. I'll take care of you until he gets here."

The rest of the night was a blur. I remember playing pool. Brett bent me over to teach me how to shoot, but it was obvious he just wanted to bend me over the table. I stuck my little ass in the air obediently, "Like this?" I smiled up at him like a little kitten in heat. Men crowded around the pool table to watch me. I felt like a star.

I remember making out with Brett at the bar. And more shots. And lots of groping. At one point, I think we lost a pool game to some guys and we had to pay them $50. They said if I flashed them, they'd call it even. So I'd shown my perky young breasts to the entire bar.

I remember wondering, fuzzily, why Jake never showed up as Brett put me back on his bike. I was way too drunk to even remember to pull my dress down like a lady. He put me in front of him so I wouldn't fall off, and the motorcycle roared off again. I grabbed the handlebars inside his strong hands and felt the wind in my face. I drunkenly yelled into the wind as we raced down the road, my hair blowing in the wind and my dress up over my hips. I had only my little thong between me and Brett's crotch.

He pulled up to a small run-down house in a bad neighborhood. There was a chain-link fence around a tiny weedy yard. He parked his bike out front and pulled me off and dragged me up the steps and inside the house. The place was a mess and we stumbled over stuff on the floor as he fumbled with my dress and pulled me to the bedroom. I lifted my arms like a good girl but he ripped the dress off me, easily tearing the thin material and dropping it to the floor. He pushed me into the bedroom in my thong, thigh-highs, choker, and heels.

Brett grabbed me by my neck and threw me face-down on the bed. He climbed on top of me. The room was spinning. I felt him reach down and pull my thong down to my ankles. I heard him unbuckle his belt. The room was spinning. His hands found my hips and pulled them up, my little bottom in the air. I felt him guide the head of his hard cock against my tiny little quivering wet pussy.

I yelped when I felt him shove it inside me. He grabbed me by my hair and drove his cock deep inside me. I cried when I felt it penetrate me – he was too big for me and it hurt. He began to drive it in and out of me while he talked to me, "Yeah, take it baby. You know you want it." I felt his powerful body pin me down to the bed, my face buried in the dirty sheets while he mounted me from behind. I whimpered in the pillow while he used me.

He was rough, riding me hard, until he exploded inside me. He moaned with satisfaction, pulled out, and collapsed on the bed next to me. I passed out.

The Morning After

I woke up in the morning with a pounding headache. I was naked except for my thigh-highs, choker, and heels and I was in a strange bed with a large naked older man. He looked up groggily and saw the blood on the sheets. "Damn, baby, why didn't you tell me you were on the rag?"

My stomach convulsed. My head throbbed and I gagged. I threw up all over his bed.

He jumped out of bed. "Goddamn it, you are a fucking hot mess, Bree."

I sat on the bed edge of the bed, crying. He got up and rubbed his eyes, looking down at me. He stood naked by the bed and his cock was level with my young face. "Clean up in here and then make me some breakfast," he ordered and stumbled to the bathroom.

I pulled the sheets off the bed and balled them up. I saw the blood. I wasn't going to tell them that it wasn't my period. I wasn't going to give him the satisfaction of knowing he'd taken my virginity. I found his shirt, a flannel long-sleeve shirt, and pulled it on and buttoned it up. I unstrapped my high heels. I could barely walk in them, especially when I was this sick. I slid my thigh highs down and threw them in the corner. I took off the choker and threw it, too, but I was so weak it just fell to my bare feet.

I went barefoot to the kitchen and threw up again, this time in the sink. I felt awful. I'd lost my virginity to a man I barely knew. I was leaning over the sink, holding back my blonde hair. Brett came up behind me and wrapped his arms around me. I shuddered when he touched me.

"Hey baby, look at this," he held his phone out. There was a picture of me smiling drunkenly and holding my dress up while some dirty biker guy knelt down and posed pointing at the little 'Princess' written on my thong with his other hand on my bare inner thigh. I threw up again.

"Wait, you had your phone last night?" I gagged.

"Hell yeah, baby. And I hung up that pay phone before you could leave the address. No way I was letting that sweet ass get away." He spanked my ass in his shirt. I jumped, and another wave of nausea hit me.

"You bastard!" I turned weakly and tried to hit him but he easily caught my hand and shoved me away.

"Damn, bitch, you need to calm down."

Suddenly it occurred to me that everyone would be really worried about me. I'd just disappeared last night. They'd be searching everywhere for me. I needed to get home immediately.

Brett reluctantly drove me back to my car. He strapped a gas can to the back of him motorcycle and I climbed on, just wearing his flannel shirt with my thong underneath. With my long bare legs, my heels on, and my hair a mess, I looked like a biker's whore on the back.

At my car, he poured gas from the can while I stood there, increasingly terrified of the trouble I'd be in with my parents. And, of course, with Jake.

He put the can down. "OK, should be good to go."

I look up at him, "What do you mean?"

"You were just out of gas, baby."

I was shocked. He'd tricked me! The whole time, he'd tricked me! I unlocked the car, shaking my head in disgust.

"What, no kiss goodbye? Give me your number, baby. I want to tap that again." He climbed on his bike, smiling, so proud of himself.

I got in my car and locked the door from the inside and flipped him the bird. I put the key in and tried to start it. It took a couple tries but it started right up. I couldn't believe it. He'd tricked me all night! I was just out of gas. And he had a phone the whole time.

I drove home knowing I was completely doomed. I thought about telling them I was raped, but what if they found Brett? He had pictures and witnesses. My head throbbed and the sunlight was killing me. I thought about telling them I was in an accident and passed out. But there was nothing wrong with the car. Finally I decided I would tell them I ran out of gas and didn't have my phone, so I slept in the car. But I couldn't go home looking like this.

Sarah to the Rescue

I decided to drive over to Sarah's house. She was a friend on the cheer team, but not a particularly close friend. But she was a hot little size zero like me and I'd loaned her some clothes one day when she'd spilled soda all over her yellow dress at lunch. I hoped to get my clothes back from her so I could wear them home. I choked down four mints I found in the car to cover my horrible vomit breath and drove to her house.

"Hi, Bree!" Sarah smiled sunnily as she opened the door. She was an adorable little brunette sophomore and she worshipped me. She desperately wanted to be the next cheer captain. Her gymnastics were really good so she had a decent chance. But today I needed her for something else: clothes. Hopefully she had mine there, or at least could loan me something that looked like it was mine. I wanted to look as normal as possible when I got home.

Sarah looked me up and down, seeing me wearing just a man's shirt with my hair in a tangled mess, and giggled, "You look like a big ol' bag of slut!" She held the door open and I walked in. We snuck up to her room. She closed the door to her room behind us and giggled excitedly, "Did Jake get lucky?!?"

I shook my head. "No, nothing like that. I just put this on because I was doing some work on my car." To anyone who knew me, the idea that I would work on my car was ridiculous. And the idea that I would leave the house in a man's old smelly flannel shirt and some stripper heels was insane. But Sarah bought it.

Sarah found my clothes in her closet. She had my cute white denim miniskirt and a nice little pink tie-front top. I breathed a sigh of relief. They were clean and folded nicely.

I looked her in the eyes, pressing my luck because I wanted her to have as little as possible to tell if she ever mentioned this to anyone, "Mind if I grab a shower? I got a lot of oil on me from the engine."

She happily agreed. I'd never been in her house and she was proud to have the head cheerleader visit. In the bathroom I saw myself in the mirror. I looked like hell. My green eyes were bloodshot and my eye shadow was smeared. I showered, finally feeling a little better. I washed a lot between my legs, wishing I could wash away the memory of Brett fucking me. I brushed my teeth over and over, trying to get the horrible taste out of my mouth. I could taste vomit and alcohol and Brett. I felt bad about using Sarah's toothbrush, but this was an emergency. I found some mouthwash and try to gargle it, but it made me want to throw up again. I got dressed in the bathroom – I didn't dare ask Sarah to borrow a bra. I came out wearing the cute miniskirt and pink top, my hair up in a ponytail. I balled up Brett's shirt and stuffed it in her bathroom trash can. I picked up my slutty stripper heels and carried them out with me.

"Thanks Sarah, you're a lifesaver!" I smiled, trying to act like my normal happy self. "We should go see a movie or something..."

She smiled excitedly. "Yeah! Do you want to meet my parents?"

"Yeah, maybe later, when I pick you up to go out?" I promised, knowing it was a lie.

I drove home. I checked myself in the mirror. I looked pretty normal except for my bloodshot eyes. But I was sure I could explain that. Surely a terrifying sleepless night in my car would make my eyes bloodshot. I decided to make up a story about a guy on a motorcycle who brought me some gas in the morning. That part was sort-of true. When I pulled up to my house, I saw Jake's car out front. And our pastor's car. And a police car. Holy shit.

I turned the car off and caught my breath. I rehearsed my story. And I prepared the ultimate weapon: I was going to burst into tears. I walked into the house. When I opened the door, I saw my mom first. She ran over and hugged me, long and close, before she started yelling, "Where the heck have you been, young lady?"

Her shout brought everyone in the house to the door. My dad, my pastor, the cops, Jake, the neighbors. Jake was wearing a white polo shirt and some khaki shorts with his hair gelled. He looked like such a boy compared to the man I'd been with last night. I started blubbering, and I didn't need to fake it. I felt like crap and I was in so much trouble that the tears came naturally.

I told them my story between tears, how I'd run out of gas on the side of the road and was too scared to walk anywhere. I'd left my purse at home so I didn't have my phone. I was so scared all night long.

They were all so concerned. They hugged me and reassured me that everything would be all right. "Well, I'm just glad you're alright," smiled one of the policemen. I was getting away with it!

Then Jake spoke up from the back, "But Bree, what about the voicemail you left me? You said I needed to pick you up, and then it just cut off. And it sounded like you were, like, in a restaurant or something?"

Oh, no! I'd completely forgotten about the phone call. But I'd been in three school plays, including the lead in 'Alice in Wonderland'. And I was in the debate club. I called on all my acting skills. With tears streaming down my cheeks, I said, "It was the worst thing! These guys pulled over. It was dark. I didn't dare get out of the car but they let me use a phone through the window. I called you..." I looked up at Jake sadly, "...but then I got scared that the guys would get out of their car so I hung up. You probably just heard them and their, uh, radio in the background."

One cop looked at me suspiciously, but his partner said, "Next time, young lady, you call us. Not your boyfriend? Understand?" I nodded my cute little blonde head. Jake looked unconvinced. My pastor put his arm around me in a friendly way, "There, there, you did the right thing staying in that car."

He started to pontificate to my parents about how a guardian angel must have watched over me all night. Yeah, right, I thought. Brett was no angel.

I excused myself and went up to my room and shut the door behind me. I listened as all the cars left. My mom brought me some herbal tea and told me to take a nap. She sat on the end of my pink bed and stroked my hair, "Bree, your dad was scared to death. We all were. And poor Jake was a mess! You need to be more careful. You know your dad has been trying to teach you car stuff for years. But we're just glad you're OK." She smiled at me gently while she stroked my hair and whispered, "I've never learned that car stuff, either."

The Aftermath

After she left, I changed out of my clothes and into some comfy pink PJs. The only things I had left from the outfit last night were the stripper heels and my Princess thong. My choker was somewhere in Brett's apartment along with my fishnet thigh-highs and the dress he ripped off of me. For some reason, I carefully hid the stripper heels in the back of my closet, but I left the thong on under my PJs. I liked the way it felt, so tiny and slutty, with the little silky strap between my cheeks. And why did it give me a thrill to think of all the men who'd seen the little 'Princess' rhinestones?

I slept for half the day. I woke up having a very intense dream – Brett was fucking me on a pool table and I was begging for more. It was so vivid. I could feel myself bent over the pool table, all the men watching, while he fucked me hard and deep. I could feel the hard edge of the pool table against me and I could feel his hard cock inside me. I sat straight up in bed. My little pussy was so wet. What was wrong with me? It was bad enough that I let a pig like Brett take my virginity; now I was dreaming about him, too? But I couldn't help it. I slid my hand down between my creamy thighs and gently rubbed my little clit. I thought about Brett picking me up and putting me on his motorcycle, spreading my legs, and taking me right there. Slowly and gently and rhythmically I rubbed my clit. My other hand fingered my tight little pussy. Soon I was moaning, my hot young body writhing under my pink bedspread until I had the most intense orgasm. I fell back on my bed. Oh, this was bad! Instead of fantasizing about a nice boy like Jake who loved and respected me, I'm fingering myself and thinking about a dirty old biker?

That evening I called Jake. It was really uncomfortable. He could tell that something had changed; something had come between us. But I couldn't stop thinking about the man who had cum inside me. Suddenly I sat up, nearly dropping the phone. I made excuses and hung up on Jake. I was scared to death. Brett had cum inside me! Jake and I had always planned on using condoms for protection. He'd been carrying them around for years. It had become a little joke between us. I always asked him if he'd checked the expiration date recently. But I was too drunk to ask Brett to wear one, and I don't think he would have listened anyway.

I was certain I was pregnant. I started feeling sick. I knew it must be morning sickness, even though it was Saturday evening. It would be so horrible – I'd be a teen mom and I'd never tell anyone who the father was. Everyone at school would think I was a total skank, even the real skanks. My parents would be disgraced. Jake would leave me. Would I even go to college? My life was over.

On Sunday, I put on some little yoga shorts and a sports bra and headed out, telling my mom I was going to work out. She looked at me worriedly and told me to be careful, even though it was broad daylight outside. I drove over to the grocery store on the opposite side of town and walked down the aisle with the feminine products. I found it immediately: a pregnancy test. I went to the self-checkout and bought it, so I wouldn't have to face a cashier. Then I turned and went back into the store and found the bathroom. I waited until the bathroom was empty and closed myself in a stall. I opened the package and read the instructions carefully. I peed on the little stick while hovering

over the toilet. Then I sat and waited.

And waited.

Then I saw the little line appear in the window.

Wait... does that mean I'm pregnant? I fumbled with

the instructions again. Oh! Not pregnant! Not

pregnant! "Yes!" I yelled out, hearing my voice echo

in the bathroom. Someone else was in the bathroom

with me now; she laughed and said, "Get it all out,

sister." I shoved the other pregnancy test in my bag

to take home with me; the instructions said that you

should test again just to be sure after a couple days.

But I was so relieved. It felt like such a weight off

my shoulders. I called my doctor while I was driving

home. I was getting on the pill immediately.

More Car Trouble

I stopped at a gas station on my way home. I was still driving on just the gallon of gas Brett put in my car. I got out to pump my gas, totally oblivious to the world around me, thinking about how lucky I was not to be pregnant. It was only after I'd swiped my card and put the pump in the tank that I noticed the man in the Porsche on the other side of the pump eyeing me. I realized that I was wearing these tiny little yoga shorts that really cling to my ass and show off my long legs. All the other girls on the cheer squad joke that the boys come to watch us practice just for my yoga shorts. And my little sports bra showed off my bare midriff; my dad hated it.

The man was older, probably in his late 20s or maybe older, and really good-looking. And he knew it. He was wearing a black suit with a v-neck t-shirt underneath and some mirrored sunglasses. Hopefully the mirrored sunglasses were meant to be ironic. He probably thought I couldn't tell he was checking me out behind the mirrors. But girls can always tell.

Before this weekend, I would have secretly enjoyed the attention, but never in a million years would I dare say anything or even meet his eyes. But today, for some reason, I was different. I smiled over at him, "Nice car."

He smiled back and took his glasses off. "Thanks. Nice... everything." I saw him look me over. He walked over to my side of the pump and took hold of the gas pump.

"A good-looking girl like you never has to pump her own gas," he smiled confidently and winked.

"My hero!" I smiled up at him like a little tease.

"So... what do you do?" he asked as he pulled the pump out of my tank and put it back.

"I'm a student -- a college student," I lied.

He looked me up and down and whistled slowly. "Lucky college. I'm going to enroll today," he smiled. "I'll pick up another degree to go with my MBA," he bragged.

"Oh good, I need a new study partner," I said with a little teasing smile across my lips.

"Turn around," he ordered. I turned around obediently, my little bottom sticking out so adorably in my yoga shorts. Why did I love forceful men all of a sudden? He put his card on my back and wrote on it, using me for a desk. I was sure he enjoyed the view.

He tucked the card in the waistband of my yoga shorts. "Text me whenever you want a ride in my

Porsche." He climbed into his bright yellow sports car and it roared to life as he drove off. I could see him watching me in his rear view mirror. He didn't take his eyes off me until he pulled into traffic. I climbed back in my car, an ancient Honda, barely able to breathe. I read the card with his number and his name, Matt. The card said he was an investment banker. What had just happened? Two days ago I was a good girl. No one would dream of tucking anything into my shorts! But it seemed like men could just read me now. Did I have 'slut' written on my forehead?

I drove home, turned on again. I imagined going out with Matt and riding in his Porsche. I'd wear another really hot dress and at then end of the night he'd nail me right on the hood of his Porsche. I had to stop thinking like this. Did this happen to all girls when they lose their virginity? I felt like a little sex

machine. I need it so badly!

Bad Girls' Dreams

Every night for the next week I dreamt about men fucking me. I'd wake up soaking wet. In my dreams, men would pin me down and pull my hair while they fucked me nice and hard and deep. They'd order me around and I'd obey. I was always a little ashamed to wake up remembering that I'd dreamt about Brett fucking me. And when I woke up, I couldn't resist touching myself. I was masturbating at least twice a day. Sometimes a lot more. I masturbated in bed in the morning, in the shower, and in bed at night. I was a sex addict. I just didn't have a man to fuck me.

Well, I did. Jake was my boyfriend and I loved him. What was wrong with me? Every girl in school was jealous of me. I had Jake, the class president and cross-country team captain and most gorgeous boy in school. But in my dreams and fantasies, it was never Jake pounding me into the bed. It was always an older, forceful man taking me. Jack could sense I wasn't in the mood and we didn't really make out – just a perfunctory kiss when he dropped me off after school because I said I had a headache or a lot of homework or needed to practice cheerleading.

Jake still drove me to school almost every day. We ate lunch together. We had 3rd period English together. But the whole experience on his birthday had really changed us. I didn't really have anything to say to him, because, honestly, the only thing that was on my mind was sex. Hot dripping wet sex. Big manly cocks jammed inside me. I even found myself in math class dropping my pencil and bending over to get it, or pretending to read while slowly crossing my long legs in my tiny skirt. But I wasn't showing off for the boys. I was showing off for our math teacher, Mr. Abrams. All the girls loved him because he was young and single and cute and he had this endearing habit of calling all the girls "Miss". I didn't love him like they did; he tried too hard to be the cool teacher. But suddenly I wanted him. At the end of class, I leaned back in my chair, my little miniskirt climbing my thighs, and made sure he got a peek at my pink panties while I stuck my pen in my mouth.

Mr. Abrams coughed when he saw me and excused the class as the bell rang. I made sure I was the last one out, but Mr. Abrams didn't dare make eye contact with me. He pretended not to notice me, digging around in his desk, until I left. I sighed. What a coward! He could have fucked the head cheerleader. I walked out, swinging my young hips in my little skirt.

I sighed again when I sat down for lunch across from Jake and between two of my friends. I realized I needed to get laid. I couldn't stop thinking about sex. I looked over at Jake. He was a really cute boy. And he really liked me. And, honestly, he'd put in years of work to get me into bed. Maybe I should just let him have what he desperately wants? That boy had to be hornier than me by now! He'd been touching me and kissing me since I was 14, and he still hadn't gotten any. Poor kid. But no. Jake just didn't do it for me. I decided to text Matt.

In 5th period math class, I held my phone under my desk and wrote out a text. And rewrote it. I wrote it over and over. I started with just, "Hi" and changed it to "'Sup?" and then thought that was stupid and childish. But I realized that he wouldn't recognize my number with any of those. He didn't even know my name. Why was I doing this? I bet he hit on a lot of girls. Finally I wrote out, "Hi Matt, it's Bree. Your new study partner from the gas station?"

I stared at it. I couldn't send it. This was all getting crazy. I'd done one really stupid thing but that didn't change who I was. I was not going out with a grown man. I needed to get back to just being me. I sighed. I guess if I just had to have sex, I could have sex with Jake. I stared down at the little screen. Despite all my reservations, I pressed 'send'. You know how they say boys think with their dicks? I was thinking with my pussy.

I couldn't pay attention for the rest of the day. It had been over a week since I met him – would he even remember me? I kept secretly checking my phone. We weren't allowed to have them in class, and in 6th period my science teacher was a total witch about it. If she caught you, she kept your phone until you brought a note from your parents. I excused myself twice to go to the bathroom during her class just to check for a text from Matt. The annoying thing was my phone kept vibrating, but it wasn't from Matt. It was always one of my friends. Or Jake. Jake texted me constantly. I used to think it was so sweet, but now I just rolled my eyes.

On the ride home, Jake talked nonstop about a party this weekend. He even dropped a really bad hint, saying, "Yeah, his parents won't be home, I bet we can find an empty bedroom..." but I ignored him. I felt my phone vibrate in my bag. I didn't dare pull it out in front of him. I was so eager to get home and see if it was from Matt. Before the car even pulled to a stop I leaned over and kissed Jake's cheek and said, "Bye!" and opened the door. He looked up, confused, but I was gone. I grabbed my backpack and had my phone in my hands as I walked up the steps.

An Older Man

Matt had texted! "Hello, hot study partner. Want to hit the books tonight?" I smiled to myself as I skipped up the stairs. I had to think of something witty to say. But something mature. And sexy. I sat on my bed with my long legs curled up under me and stared at my phone. Finally I wrote, "What do you have in mind, Porsche boy?" It wasn't witty or mature or sexy, but it was all I could think of and I couldn't wait any longer.

Instead of a text message, my phone vibrated with a phone call. Matt was calling me! Who called anymore? But then I reminded myself that he was pretty old. I guessed around 30.

"Hello?" I answered. I was so nervous. I wanted to sound cool. And older.

"Hello, beautiful, it's Matt. I thought I'd save some time with all the texting and just call you. Besides, it's hard to text-and-drive when you have a stick shift."

I smiled to myself. "Matt who?"

"You know exactly who, beautiful. And you are imprinted on my brain. But I don't know your name."

I giggled, smiling happily, squirming on my bed. I tossed my stuffed bear in the air. "I'm Bree."

"Bree? I like it. Sounds very hot. Suits you perfectly."

"Thanks." I didn't know what to say. My cheeks were flushed. I was talking to a grown man on the phone!

After an awkward pause when I wasn't sure if I should say something, he said, "Look, this is a little last-minute, but a friend of mine owns a gallery and they have an opening tonight. It's some art photography thing. Why don't you put on a little black dress and I'll pick you up? Which dorm do you live in?"

Tonight? Go out on a Thursday night? I had school tomorrow. My mom would never go for it. And I didn't live that close to the campus. But it was so exciting. Go out to an art gallery? I felt so mature. This wouldn't be Jake feeling me up in some kid's bedroom while we shared a cheap beer. I'd be on the arm of a man in an art gallery! But no, not on a school night. I couldn't do it. I had homework to do.

But I heard myself say, "What time?"

He told me the gallery opening was from 8 to midnight. He explained that his friend would have cocktails and champagne circulating until 10, so we should get there early if we want a drink.

I found myself agreeing that he could pick me up at "my" dorm, which I quickly looked up on the internet while we were on the phone, at 8 o'clock. That meant I had almost four hours to come up with an excuse to tell my parents, find a dress to wear, get ready, drive myself over to campus, find a place to park, and be waiting for him in front of the dorm. After we hung up, I realized how impossible it was. I couldn't do this! But it was so hot – a date with a grown man. And it was a real date, at an art gallery, like something out of the movies. It was so romantic!

I texted my mom immediately. I told her that I had to help my friend, Kelsey, with some urgent boyfriend drama. My mom was used to hearing about boyfriend drama from me. I asked if I could stay out late. I held my breath, sure she'd say no. It was a school night. I'd almost never been out past bedtime on a school night! Surely she'd think it was really strange. I'd used Kelsey's name because she was the most uptight of all my friends and the least suspicious. Her parents were so boring and uptight that I'd heard my mom joke once that they wouldn't need any embalming fluid for her parents when they died because they were already so uptight. But my mom texted right back, "Sure." No questions. No reminders to do my homework. Weird. I guess I could pull this off!

I went in my closet and turned on the light. This was going to be tough. I wanted to look mature, older, and hot. I was going to be riding around in a Porsche! I'd be eye candy in an art gallery! I felt like a movie star and I wanted to dress like one. But I didn't have anything in my closet that would work. I pulled out the dress I'd worn as Homecoming queen, but it was too girly, all pink with bows. And it was too long. My favorite white dress for church was way too conservative. I wanted something way up my thighs. It was just too bad Brett had destroyed my only slutty dress in his hurry to get me naked.

I didn't know what to do. Then I remembered Sarah. When I was at her house, she'd had a lot of clothes in her closet. But, even better, she had an older sister. I bet she had something tight and elegant and sexy. I'd have to talk Sarah into it. I called her immediately.

Raiding Sarah's Closet

"Sarah? I need your help!" I gushed to her about how I had a really important college admissions meeting tonight and I wanted to look grown up. I'd noticed how elegant and well-dressed she always was – could she please help me? Sarah ate it up. She was thrilled to help the most popular girl in school.

I drove over there immediately. We were in her closet in seconds. I tore through everything she had, but all her stuff was even more childish and girly than mine. Other than her cheerleading uniform, she didn't have a single dress that was above her mid-thigh. Kids! But I casually asked if her sister might have something.

"My sister?" she looked up at me, so immature, "She's not home and I'm not allowed to touch her

stuff when she's not here. Or when she is here."
Her sister was a few years older than us and I didn't really remember her from school. She was taking a semester off from college to model. She was very tall and thin, but honestly I didn't think she was the prettiest girl in the world. But men liked her.

"Can't we just look in her closet?" I begged, holding Sarah's arm and smiling excitedly.

Sarah led me over to her sister's room. We snuck in even though no one was home. Her sister had plastered the walls of her room with pictures of herself modeling. She had this awkward look on her face in every picture, but her mouth was parted the way models are supposed to pose. One of my friends described 'model mouth' as, "Part your lips like the photographer is about to stick his dick in there."

Sarah slowly opened the door to her sister's closet. Suddenly it was like the clouds parted and I could hear angels singing – the closet was jammed with clothes! Everything from long elegant ball gowns to short little black dresses. And nothing cheap, either. How could she afford this stuff? Her sister had barely gotten any real paid modeling work that I'd heard of, and that was for a local print campaign. But Sarah explained that one of her sister's friends, another model, loaned her a lot of stuff. That model had a rich older boyfriend. That's why Sarah wasn't allowed in there – the clothes weren't even her sister's.

There were a lot of good options. I looked at a tight yellow dress, a hot red dress, and a black dress that was very low-cut. But in the back of the closet, by itself, was a zipped black bag on a hanger. I slowly unzipped it. Inside was the most magical dress: it was soft black leather strapless dress with a bustier top that I was sure would make my breasts stand straight out. The skirt was very short and the whole dress was so body-fitting that I knew it would be almost constricting. It was perfect! This was not a dress for a child. It was like a work of art. I read the label: it was a real Italian designer dress. I'd seen that kind of stuff before on TV and in magazines, but never actually touched a designer dress in person.

Sarah was shaking her head no before I even gave her my puppy-dog look. "Oh please please please... it's so gorgeous!" I begged.

"No, no way!" she whined, a look of terror on her pretty little sophomore face. "That dress probably costs $500, seriously! My sister would be so mad she'd kill me, then dig me up and kill me again."

I changed tactics; instead of begging, I tried reasoning with her, "Sarah, it's in a black bag! She won't even see that it's gone! And I'll have it back tonight and she'll never ever know!"

Sarah looked like she was going to cry. I could tell she didn't want to say no to me, but she didn't want to risk death from her sister either. She was caught in the middle. Time for a third tactic: bribery.

"Sarah, if you do this for me – and it's soooo important for me – I'd feel really guilty if you didn't let me do something for you. You know, voting for Homecoming court opens in two weeks. Obviously, everyone thinks I'll win queen and Lindsay and Kylie will win the princess tiaras, but I think you'd make such a great princess. If I really really worked hard – and we'd have to keep this between us because I just love Lindsay and Kylie – I bet I could get a lot of people to vote for you. That would open a lot of eyes if a sophomore were on the court with me. It would be like passing the baton. When I graduate, someone has to step up and be cheer captain, and it will probably be someone the school recognizes..."

Lindsay and Kylie were both smoking-hot juniors. Lindsay was tall and thin and had the most gorgeous raven-black hair that fell to her shoulders. Kylie was shorter but super-athletic. Our squad could toss her really high into the air because she was really light, and she could do amazing flips. She was an adorable little brunette and had the most cheerful personality ever. Kylie texted me almost every morning just to say 'Good morning, I love you!'

Sarah was hot, too, but almost every boy in the school who wasn't in love with me was in love with either Lindsay or Kylie. It would be nearly impossible for Sarah to win. And Lindsay and Kylie, as juniors, would obviously be next in line for cheer captaincy after I graduate. I was promising Sarah the impossible. But I saw her eyes widen. I could tell she was imagining herself on homecoming court, walking out on the football field in front of everyone, and being crowned with her princess tiara next to me at the homecoming dance. And then strutting the halls of our school as a homecoming princess and future cheer captain. The wheels were turning.

"Bree, you'd have to be soooo careful..."

I'd done it. I hugged Sarah so close, our bodies pressed together. "Oh Sarah I love you!" I giggled.

I took the dress into Sarah's bathroom. I stripped off my clothes until I was just wearing my little white 'Princess' panties. Every time I saw them, I remembered my night as a biker slut. There was always little shame and revulsion when I thought about Brett and the men in the bar, but it was so hot.

My 'Princess' panties made me feel like a wild girl. I stepped into the black dress carefully and pulled it up my body, wiggling my little hips. I called Sarah to help me get dressed. She zipped me into the skin-tight dress, giggling about homecoming court. But I couldn't believe the transformation – in the Italian dress, I was a supermodel! It clung to my body, showing off every curve, and held out my breasts like a little present I was offering. Sarah helped me do my hair and makeup. We borrowed her sister's makeup and I made my eyes super dark and smoky and my cheekbones pink.

Only one problem left: shoes! I had my 6" clear stripper heels hidden in the car, but they totally wouldn't go with this elegant dress. We went back to Sarah's sister's closet and dug around until we found a sky-high pair of shiny silvery heels. They must have cost a fortune. They were a little big for me but Sarah helped me put a pad in that helped a little.

Sarah looked at me and sighed, "Oh my God you're gorgeous! I mean, isn't it a little much for college admissions?" With my dark eyes, bright red lips, long bare legs, and hot body poured into a designer dress all on top of super-high elegant heels, I felt so seductive. I was a boy's wet dream in heels. I assured her that it was really important that I look mature for this meeting. She looked a little dubious but wished me luck.

I walked out to my car, feeling so sexy and exotic and sultry in my outfit. I was so lucky I had Sarah. I couldn't ask my real friends for help – they'd see right through me if they saw me suddenly dressing like a little sex kitten. I was going to have to get a lot closer to Sarah. I could use her to keep my new life secret.

An Art Lesson

I drove over to the college campus and parked my car behind the dorms. It was resident-only parking but I was so late already. It was 8:15. I walked out to the front of the dorm. Some boys walked by and stared. It occurred to me that I probably looked pretty exotic – a girl dressed up like this on a college campus? I felt so wild, so naughty. I couldn't help smiling. When I got to the front of the dorm, I saw a familiar bright yellow Porsche sitting out front. Matt was waiting for me! I walked over, trying to hide how giddy I felt. He got out of his car and walked around to open my door like a gentleman.

He put his arm around me and gave me a little kiss on my cheek. "You look spectacular," he smiled down at me. He put his hand on my back guided me into his car. He walked around to his door and climbed in next to me.

He looked at me for a second and smile spread over his face. "Wow, you really are beautiful." He put the car in gear and we pulled out, and then his hand settled on my bare thigh. I felt my heart pound in my chest. But I wasn't going to let him grope me right away like Brett did. I put my hand on his and pulled it up. He wrapped his hand in mine and smiled over at me. I held hands with him and he settled our hands into my lap. I was holding hands with Matt! Every time he shifted gears, he would put his hand back on my thigh, and I would pick it up again. It was a little game we played the entire drive.

He kept looking over at me as he drove. "Keep your eyes on the road, mister," I smiled flirtatiously.

"Impossible," he smiled confidently as he eyed my legs. "You ever heard how they always say that Barbie dolls present an anatomically impossible body type? Well, with your tiny waist and your perfect skin and your curves, you really look like a living doll."

I smiled proudly; I'd never been compared to a Barbie doll before. The next time he shifted, I let him keep his hand on my thigh. I felt his hand on my bare skin. He confidently put his hand firmly on my thigh, taking possession, with his fingers slipping between my thighs. He was almost at the hemline of my short dress. I could barely breathe with his hand just inches from my panties.

He smiled at me and looked me directly in my eyes with his hand on my thigh at a stoplight. I tried not to blush. I was on a date with a grown man! I tried to think of something mature to talk about. "Umm, how's work?"

He laughed. "Work is work. Play is more fun." He squeezed my thigh as the light changed and he reluctantly let go to shift gears. His hand found my thigh again immediately, this time just a little bit higher up my leg.

After we parked, he walked me into the gallery. He smiled down at me as we walked in and whispered, "Those bare shoulders are so mesmerizing." He slid his hand gently along my shoulder and then down my bare back. He guided me in with his hand on my lower back, just above my bottom. I felt so special. I must have been glowing!

The gallery was small and packed with people. There was a very provocative art exhibit on – an apparently famous photographer that I'd never heard of was there, and they were displaying his photographs from a series on the modern city. But all the photos were of hot models in really odd places, like a beautiful topless girl wearing nothing but an apron and holding a pie standing in a city bus stop next to some old guy who looked homeless. I didn't get it. But the crowd was so well-dressed and hip and cool! I felt like I belonged. I felt like a grown woman.

Matt introduced me to his friend who owned the gallery. He handed me a glass of champagne and looked me over. "Need a job in a gallery?" he smiled. Matt punched him playfully.

"This one is mine," he smiled. I beamed.

I stood there with them looking at the photograph of the model and the homeless guy, thinking I could be a model. I wondered if she got a lot of money for taking off her top. Did she have to stand there in public where people could see her during the photo shoot? Was that a real homeless guy next to her, or another model?

As I stood there, a man turned to me and asked, "What do you see?" I looked up at him and realized it was the artist himself. He had piercing blue eyes and wore black jeans and a black tshirt under a wrinkled black jacket that looked like it had been balled up in the trunk of his car for a week. But he was good-looking in a starving artist kind of way and had an exciting air about him. I stammered, "It's really nice!"

"Nice? You think it's nice? This is my soul screaming out about the juxtaposition of soulless consumerist demand for crap no one needs and the actual human need that abounds in our crumbling urban cores, and you think it's 'nice'?" he practically shouted. He locked his menacing eyes on me. People around us stopped and stared. If we weren't in an art gallery, I'd be terrified that he'd hit me, or worse. I felt Matt's arm slip around me. Matt and the artist eyed each other and then Matt led me away.

Matt tried to calm me down; he got me another glass of champagne and told me that the artist was well-known for his outbursts. Most people thought it was just a clever marketing ploy, pretending to be a crazy artist. But people came to his openings, anyway, expecting some fireworks. "That whole speech he gave you about 'soulless consumer' bullshit sounded rehearsed to me," Matt reassured. But I could barely keep from crying; I felt like everyone was staring at me, and not because of my dress this time.

I didn't know that Matt was very experienced at seducing young women; he knew just when to be aggressive and when to relax me with compliments and smiles. He treated me like a skittish little baby deer. And he could tell it was time to take me out of the gallery. He led me out to his car and opened the door for me. I saw him watch as I climbed in; the Porsche was very low to the ground so my dress slid up as I got in. He obviously enjoyed the show. I tugged my little dress down after I was in my seat. He closed the door and went around to his side.

He smiled gently at me. I felt a little better now that we were out of the gallery. He leaned over and put the gentlest little kiss on my lips. I smiled back at him. And then he kissed me again, this time with real passion, our tongues meeting. We separated and smiled at each other. I felt flush. He was so confident and exciting and older.

As he started the car, he smiled back at me. "Wow... our first kiss." I smiled up at him, bursting with happiness. I imagined he'd be my boyfriend now. I couldn't exactly bring him home to my parents, and he thought I was a college girl, so it would be pretty complicated. I'd started our entire relationship on a lie. And we hadn't even really had a conversation yet about anything, and I didn't really know anything about him, but it was so exciting to think about dating a man. A real man.

As we pulled off, he put his hand back on my thigh. "When you got in, I couldn't help noticing something," he smiled. "Your dress slid up a little and I saw the cutest white panties peeking out."

"Oh!" I blushed, covering my face with my hands and laughing.

"And there was something written on them," he smiled, his hand on my thigh again, even further up my dress. So close to the panties he was describing. "What does it say?" he laughed with me.

"You'll never know!" I joked.

"Never? Never? You're killing me!" he pretended to die, swerving the car in the other lane. I laughed with him.

"Hmmm... let me guess: does it say "'Closed until Wedding Day'?"

"No." I smiled cutely up at him.

"Whew. Because otherwise I'd have to get us on a flight to Vegas tonight for a quickie wedding."

"I meant yes! It says 'Closed until Wedding Day'!" I gushed. We laughed together again, our eyes meeting briefly. His hand explored my thigh. I kept waiting for him to get too high up my dress, but he seemed to know exactly how far he could go.

He pulled the car into the parking lot under a high-rise building. He drove down two levels and pulled into a reserved parking spot. "Where are we?" I smiled.

"Home," he smiled back, leaning in for another kiss. I kissed him back, feeling the stubble on his face against my smooth skin. But I realized he'd just taken me to his house. I wanted to have sex – I wanted to have sex so badly – but I didn't want to be a slut. I knew he was a grown man and I'd watched enough TV to know that he'd expect me to crawl into bed with him. But I didn't want to be a one-night stand. I wanted to be his girlfriend! I wasn't sure what to do.

But on the elevator on the way up to his condo, he pinned me against the wall, kissing me while his hands found my ass. I kissed him back and felt him grind his hips against me. The elevator doors opened but he wouldn't stop kissing me, so the door closed and started back down. He pulled away and we both laughed as we rode the elevator all the way back down.

"Let's try that again," he whispering in my ear as he punched the button and we kissed again. This time he held my hips firmly while he kissed me. I was dizzy by the time the door opened and I'd barely had a glass and a half of champagne. I was drunk on Matt.

He led me into his condo. I caught my breath when I walked in; the condo had floor-to-ceiling windows that looked out over the city. With the city lit up at night, it was really spectacular. "Beautiful view," he said. I nodded my little blonde head and looked over at him and grinned when I realized he was talking about me. His eyes slowly slid up my body. I felt a chill down my spine and that familiar warmth between my legs.

I knew he'd start to seduce me now. He had me

alone in his condo. It was dark and so romantic and

we'd been kissing. But I was determined not to be a

slut. I wasn't going to sleep with him on our first

date, no matter how badly I needed a good fuck.

An Entirely Different Lesson

Matt left me looking out the window and went to the kitchen. He brought back two glasses of wine and handed me one. "Cheers!" he smiled. I smiled back and touched glasses, but my guard was up. This was all new to me, but I had to find a way to let him know that I liked him without sleeping with him. It was the right thing to do.

But instead of putting the moves on me, he asked, "So what do you want to do? Watch a movie?" He stood next to me, looking out the window, sipping his wine. He didn't even touch me. I was a little insulted – I was sure he'd have his hands all over me. He couldn't keep his hand off my leg in the car and he'd groped me in the elevator. But now he just stood there?

"Uh, yeah, a movie? That sounds... nice." It did sound nice! Maybe he was just a really nice respectful kind of guy. He didn't just expect me to crawl into bed right away.

We sat on the white leather couch together. Close together. He got the remote and flipped through the movies he had recorded. He looked over at me when he got to an action movie. I shook my head no. He looked over at me when he got to a romantic comedy and I nodded. He clicked on it. I smiled up at him.

He put his arm around me and our faces were so close. I was ready to give him a little speech about how I'm not ready for sex, when he said, "Listen, before we start the movie, do you want to change into something more comfortable? Don't get me wrong, I love seeing that dress climb up your thighs, but trust me, you've already impressed me. We could just put on some comfortable clothes and watch a movie, you know, like friends?"

"Really?" I smiled with relief. "This dress is sooo tight! It's hard to sit in it." And secretly I was worried about spilling something on it.

He smiled back, "Yeah, I think that dress was made for strutting down runways, not curling up on couches."

He got up and went to his bedroom. I wasn't sure where this was all going, but he really seemed nice. He came back with a package, "This is something I was going to give to my niece, but it'll probably fit you," he said as he handed it to me. "I thought it might be a little too forward to give you one of my shirts, even though you'd look spectacular curled up on my couch in one of my shirts."

I smiled so happily up at him. He was so sweet. I looked down at the package. "Girls pajamas?" I looked up at him dubiously.

He laughed, "Yeah, I got them for my niece. I figured that's what a 12-year-old girl would like. Lots of pink and lace and stuff, right? But it should fit you, it says on the package that it has some stretchy material, so it should stretch for the parts of you that aren't, you know, 12-years-old." He nodded towards his bedroom. "You can go first."

I took the pajamas and walked into his bedroom. He had a giant king-sized bed and the room was immaculate. His bedroom was furnished with a huge heavy dresser and a big luxurious leather chair, but a big bed dominated the room. He had a beautiful off-white duvet and matching pillows. It was the kind of bed you wanted to curl up and sleep for days. But I was pretty sure that if Matt had his way I wouldn't get much sleep in that bed. It turned me on to stand by the bed, knowing that someday soon Matt would take me to bed right there. But not today!

I opened the bag containing the pajamas. There was a little pink pair of boxer shorts with hearts on them and a matching tank top. But it was just too small for me. But I was a little worried about drinking wine on the couch in Sarah's sister's dress. I didn't dare get it dirty. So I decided to put on the pajamas. I kicked my heels off – my feet were killing me – and took off the dress carefully and put it over his chair. I thought he might like seeing my dress on the chair in his bedroom. I saw myself in his mirror over his dresser just wearing my little white 'Princess' panties and remembered that he was dying to read them. I smiled to myself.

I wasn't wearing a bra, so when I tugged on the little tank top it stretched over my breasts, squeezing them together. My hard nipples stood out prominently. And the shirt was too short to cover my smooth hard flat belly. I stepped into the little boxer shorts but they were so tight and so short that I could see my cute little cheeks peeking out. No 12-year-old girl could make these PJs look like this. I wasn't sure I wanted to go out like this. I saw one of his sweatshirts in his closet and pulled it on, but when I saw myself in the mirror I changed my mind. Matt was so respectful and he really seemed to like me; what would it hurt to give him a little show? But I had to be very careful not to end up in bed with him. I promised myself I'd be a good girl, even if I looked like a very bad one.

I walked out wearing the little pajamas. Matt looked up from the couch and then fumbled the remote.

"Whoa." His eyes found my perky breasts. "Are you smuggling grapefruit in that top?"

I giggled and covered my breasts with my hands and stuck my tongue out at him. "If you're not going to be nice, I'm going to find a blanket."

He stood up and wrapped his arms around me, "Oh, my darling, I am so sorry. So terribly sorry! I would never mean to offend your perfect breasts." He laughed. I smiled up at him and giggled, feeling so hot. He left to get changed and came back wearing boxers and a tshirt. He sat down next to me and started the movie. I couldn't believe he wasn't turned on now; why wasn't he trying to drag me off to bed? But I sat on the couch next to him quietly. He sipped wine and laughed, nudging me at parts of the movie. But where was the touching and making out I expected? I was so confused.

I reached up to put my hair down. Matt watched me put my hair in a ponytail. He smiled, "You're such a doll. I could watch you forever." I felt his arm around my shoulders. He pulled me closer and I leaned my head on his shoulder. I felt him kiss the top of my head. I turned and tilted my head back, wanting a kiss. A real kiss. Matt knew exactly what to do.

He kissed me passionately, deeply, our bodies intertwined on the couch. He pulled me into his lap. Soon I was straddling him and I could feel his cock growing between my legs. He took my face in his hands and looked up at me, our eyes meeting. He kissed my lips softly, then my cheeks, eyes, forehead. His mouth found my ear and nibbled gently. Then he moved on to my neck. I found myself gently grinding my hips against him. His kisses were magic.

He slowly tugged my shirt up and pushed me back on the couch. He kissed my bare belly. He kissed down my legs to my feet. Then he sucked each of my toes. At first I giggled and squirmed but soon I was moaning softly as he sucked my toes. Then he moved up and tugged my shirt up higher and smiled, "Hands up." I lift my arms for him like a good girl and he peeled off my top. His mouth found my nipples immediately and he licked and sucked and nibbled until I was a mewling little kitten in heat. I squirmed on the couch under him, trembling with excitement, my young body out of control.

I was naked except for the little boxers he'd given me, but I'd lost all self-control. When his hands found the waistband of my little snug boxers, I instinctively lifted my hips for him to pull them off. He smiled down at me. "Princess?" he smiled as he looked at my little white thong. "I love it!" he slowly rubbed my little thong. I'm sure he could tell how wet I was. He leaned down and kissed my thong, right over my quivering wet pussy.

"Oh!" I moaned softly, arching my back on the couch. My long thin legs spread a little wider for him. He gently slid the thong aside, and his tongue very gently licked my clit. He spread my legs, his hands firmly on my thighs, and his head between my legs. I gripped the couch with my hands, my whole body tensing. I'd never felt anything like this before. He expertly licked and sucked my clit, and soon his finger found my wet pussy. I closed my eyes tight as I felt a wave overcome me. I had the best orgasm of my life, moaning and squirming helplessly and collapsing on the couch.

What Men Want

Matt scooped me up in his arms and carried me to his bed. I was beyond resisting. I put my arms around his neck, my naked body surrendered to him. He put me gently on the bed and climbed in next to me. He kissed me softly and he he peeled off his tshirt and boxers. We kissed, our naked bodies pressed together, his manly body on top of mine.

He slid up the bed until his hard throbbing cock was level with my mouth. I knew what to do; I'd practiced at home for years on cucumbers, bananas, and anything else I could find that was about the size and shape of a cock. He pushed his cock into my mouth, feeding it to me, and I wrapped my warm wet mouth around the head. I started to gently suck on his cock, looking up at him. He grinned down at me, "I love that little mouth." He moaned while he slowly pushed it in and out of my mouth. I kept my lips wrapped around it, sucking.

He started forcing it a little deeper, sliding it in and out. He grabbed my hair, making me take it. I didn't resist, trying to take it deep like the girls in the porn videos I'd seen online. But it was so big and so deep that I gagged, and he seemed to like making me gag. He shoved it deeper and faster, gagging me on it. He pulled it out and I gasped for air.

He slid down and put the head of his cock, wet with my saliva, against my little wet pussy. I remembered I wasn't going to have sex with him, but it was too late. He pressed gently, pushing himself inside me. Soon he pulled my legs around his waist and pinned my hands above my head on the bed and began to drive his hips, shoving his cock into me. I was helpless, pinned down to the bed, unable to move. And he was fucking me hard. I heard the slap of skin on skin as he drove his hips faster and faster, fucking me.

I closed my eyes, trying to take it like a good girl. But it was rough – he was really pounding me into the bed. I bit my lip, but I let out one little yelp when he really jammed it deep inside me. He liked that yelp, and I got it harder and harder after that. I couldn't help it; I yelped and cried, "Matt, it hurts!" That was all it took: I could feel him convulse as he exploded inside me. He collapsed on top of me.

After he caught his breath, he smiled down at me and kissed me. "Wow," he smiled, "you're a wild little Princess, aren't you?"

After a few minutes in bed together, softly running my hand over his chest, I explained to him that I had a really early class and couldn't spend the night.

He was reluctant to let me escape but he finally agreed to drive me back to campus. I carefully picked up the dress and my heels, but I put the little girlie PJs back on. I had a change of clothes in my car; after Matt dropped me, I'd just run around the dorm in these pajamas, hopefully without being seen, and hop in my car. With any luck, I'd drop the dress off at Sarah's and be home before midnight. My mom wouldn't like it, but I was never out that late, so I was sure she'd forgive me.

For once, everything went according to plan. Matt drove me back and dropped me off with a long passionate kiss. I got to my car without being seen. When I turned my car on, I had to laugh: the clock said 11:15. Wow, I was easy. Less than three hours into our first date and he'd already nailed me and sent me home. I drove to Sarah's and she ran out to grab the dress; she wanted to talk about our homecoming strategy but I told her I just had to get home. I promised we'd spend some time together at school. When I got home, my mom didn't say a word when I came in. She'd left out some lasagna; I hadn't eaten and I'd worked up quite an appetite.

But school the next day didn't go according to plan. On my way to school in Jake's car, I kept openly checking my texts. But I got nothing from Matt. I couldn't believe it – we'd slept together on our first date. Surely he'd text me and maybe even ask for my address to send flowers. I planned on telling him I was going home to see my parents for the weekend; that would explain what I was doing there. Maybe he could pick me up from there on our next date. It was close enough to campus that it was believable that I'd spend a lot of time there.

But my thoughts about Matt were interrupted. I got

a text. In fact, I got a lot of texts. Just none from

Matt.

Social Disaster

I stared down at my phone, my mouth open in shock. Most of the texts included a photo that was apparently all over school already: a girl laying on a bar with her skirt up over her hips while a dirty biker did a body shot off her belly button. And she seemed to be enjoying it. *I* seemed to be enjoying it. I was shocked. Where the hell did they get this photo? I was doomed.

I was red-faced as I walked into school with Jake. Jake was oblivious; he hadn't checked his phone yet. But he'd see it soon enough. All eyes seemed to be on me. I was terrified. My secret life was exposed for everyone to see! I would be cast out with the rest of the sluts and skanks. There is no way I would be homecoming queen, and my cheer captaincy would be in jeopardy. Mrs. Simpson, our cheer coach, expected all of us girls to be 'virtuous', in her words, and she set standards for grades and behavior. I'm pretty sure slutting around a biker bar wouldn't meet her standards.

I could feel the eyes of the school on me. I could hear the hum of the crowd around me. Our school was like a beehive and I was their queen. But this queen was about to be dethroned.

But I needed have worried. It was Sarah who saved me. She texted back, "Obvious photoshop. Lame." Lindsay repeated it and soon all my friends chimed in, saying it was rude and cruel to make such an obvious fake. I worked up some tears in the girls' bathroom and soon I had everyone's sympathy. "Everyone hates me!" I cried. Girls surrounded me, telling me the photo originated with some burnout loser who smoked cigarettes under the bleachers at lunch. "Who?" I asked. "A kid named Finn who wears that stupid leather biker jacket," said Tamara at lunch. I made a note of it.

At lunch I found Finn under the bleachers. He had a bright shining black eye that Jake had given him. He was a big dark-haired guy with a broad chest. Pretty brave of Jake to punch him. Jake was strong and athletic but I wouldn't call him tough. Jake was more of a pretty boy. Finn looked like a bad boy. I found out later that Jake and three other boys had cornered Finn alone in the bathroom. I confronted this Finn kid. "Where'd you get the photo?" I demanded.

"My brother Brett," he taunted, "he fucked your brains out."

"Your... your brother?" Brett had to be in his mid-30s. How could he have a brother in high school? And why did he have to be in my high school?

"Yeah, my half-brother," he smiled at me cagily.

"And you actually believe that bullshit?" I eyed him. He was a tough-looking senior that I vaguely remembered from some classes. He was good-looking in a dangerous way. "No one else will believe it. And I'll make sure you get a lot worse than a black eye if you don't admit you faked it."

"What are you going to do?" he asked calmly.

"Simple, dumbass – I'm going to whip up some tears and tell the principal that you drugged me and raped me. That photo will prove it. Have fun in prison!" I tried to act confident. He had to back down.

"You wouldn't," he said, but I could tell he knew I wasn't bluffing.

"Now, got any more photos I need to know about?" I asked.

He nodded and showed me on his phone. That fucking bastard Brett. He must have taken ten photos of me. Good thing he was drunk and stupid, because you really couldn't tell it was me except for the one Finn had spread around the school.

"Here's what you're going to do: send another text and admit you photoshopped it. Say it was just a joke. And delete all the others. If you do that, I'm going to give you a little reward: I'm not going to let everyone kick your ass no matter how much you deserve it."

After lunch, I got a note in class summoning me to the principal's office. What fresh hell was this? But when I got there, the school counselor met me first with a hug, "Oh, Bree, I'm so sorry. You must be so upset!" Great. They'd seen the picture, too? One night drunk and slutty in a bar and suddenly I'm the poster-child for body shots?

Finn, the kid that sent the picture around the school, was already in the principal's office, nursing his black eye. He looked up calmly when I walked in. Wasn't he afraid I going to accuse him of rape? If he was, he didn't show it. The principal, assistant principal, school counselor, and my cheer coach, Mrs. Simpson, all joined us. They glared at Finn and our principal, a stern older black woman named Mrs. Jones, demanded an explanation.

Finn explained quietly that it was a fake, a photoshop fake that he'd made. It was just intended as a joke. Then he surprised me: he told them he'd been in love with me since 3rd grade and I'd never paid any attention to him. He was just glad that I finally knew his name. "I know I'd never have a chance with a girl as popular and pretty as Bree. I was just looking at her picture and I got the idea to put her face on this other girl..." he slumped in his chair sadly.

That disarmed the mob. They'd decided that he was the villain before anyone had gotten to the office. The boy was always the villain. But hearing him say he loved me? The principal, who had looked ready to expel Finn, softened. "Finn, thank you for your honesty. But what you did was awful and can't be undone."

Her tone changed when she turned to me, "Bree, I know cyber-bullying like this can be so damaging to a girl's self-image. Do you want to say anything to this... this... this boy?"

I turned to Finn and sniffed, "I... I do know your name, Finn. I think this is all... all my fault. I've just trying so hard to be popular that I forgot to be nice." I buried my face in my hands. It was clear to me that both Finn and I were playing roles. I peeked out and saw a little smirk on Finn's face. He'd been playing the system long enough that he wasn't intimidated by the principal. Or me. Or anyone.

The principal gave Finn a week's worth of detention. That was a wrist-slap for a repeat offender like Finn. "And smoking will kill you!" she called out as we exited her office. The school counselor handed me a stack of materials on bullying and her cell phone number, insisting I call her anytime, day or night, if I needed to talk.

Finn and I walked out of the office together. I couldn't help being impressed – he was calm under pressure. I guessed there was more to this boy than his burnout reputation would imply. We stopped in the hallway and looked at each other. He towered over me, but I felt like we were equals. We understood each other. "Well-played, loser," I smiled up at him. "Yeah, well-played, skank." He turned to go back to class, then turned back with a smile, "You looked better in that slutty dress than in this shit," he nodded toward my outfit. I was wearing a crisp white button-down top that was modestly buttoned all the way up and tucked neatly into my knee-length gray skirt. I had a white headband hold back my blonde hair and I wore tasteful soft pink lipstick. I smiled as I walked away – for some reason, it turned me on to think of Finn looking at me like that.

Working the Crowd

I went to the party with Jake that Friday night for two reasons: first, Matt never texted me, and second, I needed to play the victim. Jake had reluctantly told half the boys in school that my virginity was still intact (and, as far as he knew, it was) and the rest were convinced that it was a clever photoshop. But I could still get some miles out of this scandal.

I spent the party with my arm around Sarah, telling everyone that she was the only one that defended me. "She told everyone it was a photoshop – everyone else believed it was real!" Everyone insisted it wasn't true, that no one had believed it, but I dabbed at my eyes and insisted that Sarah was my savior. Jake tried to get in on the action, insisting that he'd gotten revenge for me, but I told everyone to leave poor Finn alone. "He's probably just so lonely and desperate for attention. It's not his fault. It's my fault. I hope no one is mean to that poor boy! I've been a terrible vice president of the student council and a terrible cheer captain!" Secretly I was intrigued by Finn.

I was surrounded all night. Everyone tried to cheer me up. Halfway through the evening, after everyone had a few drinks, I started my campaign: "Everyone knows Lindsay and Kylie will win homecoming princess voting. I just hope someone votes for Sarah, too, to show the school how important it is to stand up to bullies!" Sarah positively glowed, but I'd coached her to insist that she couldn't possibly win because Lindsay and Kylie were so glamorous and beautiful and popular. Even Lindsay and Kylie nodded their dumb little heads. My plan was underway.

Only Jake was glum. He was hoping tonight was the night, but he couldn't get me away from the crowd.

He expected that after he'd defended my honor and chastity by punching Finn, he might get to violate my honor and chastity by fucking me on some borrowed bed at a high school party. I really felt sorry for him; he was a cute boy and so loyal to me. But he was just a boy.

The Invitation

The next day Matt still hadn't texted. I knew I shouldn't, but I texted him: "Hi!" Short and simple. Not too desperate. After I sent it, I wished I'd left the exclamation point off. But no answer. I was so mad. I was not some little one-night stand! But I kept thinking it over: he'd met me at a gas station. Yeah, he'd taken me out to a gallery, but we only stayed about 15 minutes before I made a big embarrassing scene. Then he took me to his place and had me naked on his bed in an hour. Maybe he did think I was just a little tramp? But he'd been so nice to me! I felt so confused. And horny. I dreamt about Matt and Brett every night. I'd wake up and give myself an orgasm while dreaming about one of them – or both of them at the same time -- taking me right there in my pink frilly bed.

Finally, on Tuesday afternoon, after I'd completely given up, I got a text from Matt: "Busy?" That's it after five days? Five days after you nail me on our first date and you say 'busy'? I knew I should wait a day or longer before I texted back. Or never text back at all. Matt was a prick. I stared at it. What did it mean? It had to mean that he wanted to see me. And today. If I wait a day, maybe he wouldn't want to see me. Or he'd be 'busy'. After fifteen nervous minutes, I texted back, "Why?"

"Having a little party tonight."

A party? Matt was throwing a party tonight? And he wanted me there? That would mean he would introduce me to his friends! That would mean I was more than just a fuck-toy. He really did like me!

I texted back, "What should I wear?" I held my breath. I didn't have any clothes. Nothing at all!

Just a closet full of girl's clothes. Was I supposed to wear a pink dress with a white bow that I wore to church?

"I'll pick something up for you. Size 0, right?"

I was excited but nervous. He was going to buy me an outfit? But what? He had good taste in cars and furniture and stuff, but the last time he'd dressed me, I'd ended up wearing a 12-year-olds pink pajamas. What would he do to me this time? But I didn't have much of a choice. I wanted to look mature. But shopping was so hard – I was a size 0 in most brands, but sometimes a zero was just too tight up top because of my perky breasts. We agreed that I would meet him at his place before the party so I could get dressed.

When I got there, the doorman sent me up the elevator. I could tell he liked my white denim miniskirt and baby blue top. I'd done my hair and makeup myself. I felt like I looked young but it was the closest thing I had to a college girl outfit. I rode the elevator up, checking my makeup in the mirrored ceiling. I was so excited!

The Princess Party

When Matt opened the door, he swept me into his arms and kissed me. I wrapped my arms around his neck and kissed him back. He pinned me against the wall and pulled my legs up around his hips, kissing me all over my neck and ears. I smiled and giggled and squirmed in his arms. He put me down and smiled at me. I blushed. He was so hot!

"We've got to get ready!" he turned to the kitchen. I followed him in; he had bottles of wine on the countertop and bags of food. He'd obviously picked up food from some restaurant. He explained while he unpacked that he was having a business dinner with some clients and some of his business associates.

"It's going to be so fucking boring, but I figured out exactly what I need to spice it up: some eye candy!" he smiled over at me while I pulled food out of bags.

I was happy, but nervous. At the art gallery, I'd said exactly the wrong thing and everyone knew it. It was so obvious that I didn't belong there, and Matt had to take me home almost immediately. How was I going to survive a business dinner with grown-ups?

"But Matt, what will I have to say to them? I don't know anything about investment banking!" I pouted.

He grabbed my ass and kissed the back of my neck. "Kitten, all you need to do is look hot and nod at whatever they say. They'll love you." I felt a little heat between my legs when he called me 'kitten'. After we'd laid out the food and Matt opened the wine so it could "breath", whatever that meant, he pointed me toward his bedroom. "Your dress is waiting for you."

On his bed – the bed I'd shared with him – I found a dress. My mouth fell open. There was no way I was wearing this. The dress was pink velvet with little flowers in silver glitter on a front panel. It had shimming organza puff sleeves and a frilly overskirt. There were glittery silver metallic accents on the hem and sleeves. The dress had a pink velvet front and back bodice sides with big pink diamond-shaped rhinestones at the waist and a separate white petticoat with two tiers of tulle. Accompanying it was a rhinestone tiara on silver band and long pink stretch satin gloves.

It was a girl's princess dress.

I stormed back out. "Matt, what the hell? That's not a business party dress!" My lip quivered. I was going to cry.

But Matt just laughed. "I know! Look, my client is a major costume manufacturer. This is one of their most expensive costumes. Believe it or not, people buy $400 princess dresses for their kids. You'd really be doing me a major solid." His eyes locked on mine and I melted. He was wearing trim-cut gray slacks, a tight white shirt over his solid chest, and a modern black jacket. His stubble made him look like a model. So gorgeous. How could I refuse him?

Now that I knew it was important for his business, I went back and got dressed. The dress was really beautiful and obviously expensive. The dress was too snug on top, though, and my breasts were pouring out. The petticoat billowed out but stopped at the knee. I put on the little tiara and slid the long satin gloves up my arms. I saw myself in the mirror: it really was a gorgeous dress. Nothing like the cheap Princess dresses they sell at Halloween. But I looked like a slutty Cinderella. The bodice cinched my tiny waist and my breasts were barely covered. The bodice was so snug that I couldn't wear a bra underneath. There just wasn't enough room.

I walked out to Matt, excited to have him see me. I smiled and spun around for him. "Well?" I smiled. He came over to me and took my gloved hand, "Hello, Princess!"

"What about shoes?" I smiled up at him.

He shook his head, "No, no shoes. Barefoot is better. A barefoot princess!"

I shrugged. He told me that we were the hosts, so I should be prepared to pour wine for the men and serve appetizers. Matt taught me how to pour wine, twisting the bottle a little bit at the end of the pour so it doesn't drip and only filling the glass about a quarter of the way up. We drank a glass together after we practiced and then he kissed me. Soft and gentle at first, then harder and more urgent. He pulled me closer and we made out in the kitchen. When we pulled apart, he patted my ass in my princess dress and sent me off to the bathroom to fix my pink cherry lip gloss. "Hurry, kitten, they'll be here soon!"

I heard a knock on the door and I walked out to stand by Matt. Matt introduced me as "Princess Bree" to a group of five men who arrived together. I shook each of their hands. An old balding man leered at me, "Is that the 224? Alan, is that the 224?" The men studied me and Matt ordered me to spin around for them. I obeyed, showing off the dress.

The old man laughed at Matt, "You get some hot young piece of tail in my best costume and you think you'll get to underwrite my offering?" Matt laughed and shrugged, "Hey, couldn't hurt, right?" All the men laughed and moved into the living room. Matt had them all sit on the couch and chairs. There was no room for me to sit, so I stood beside Matt, trying not to look nervous.

While the men talked, a chubby man in a pin-striped suit at the end of the couch touched my elbow and looked up at me, "I love your feet! What color nail polish is that?" I leaned down and whispered, "It's called Dreamy. It's my favorite pink nail polish!"

"Oh, now it's my favorite, too," his eyes locked on my bare feet. I realized that when I leaned down to whisper, my breasts were barely contained. But he didn't look down my dress; he was totally absorbed with my bare feet. "Dreamy..." he repeated. It occurred to me that Matt must have known that this guy liked girls' feet. He had me barefoot on purpose!

"Princess Bree, why don't you see if anyone would like some wine?" Matt asked with a wink. I smiled back at him. I loved seeing him in action. He was so self-assured. Hearing him talk business was such a turn-on. I brought the wine bottle out and poured for the men. I made sure to bend over a little, showing off my breasts. I was going to help Matt close this deal!

The old man turned to me after a few glasses of wine. "Bree, sorry -- Princess Bree -- do you mind if I ask you a few product research questions?" I nodded my little tiara-covered blonde head, but I was nervous about speaking. I didn't want to embarrass Matt.

He asked me about the fit of the dress. I lied and said it fit perfectly; the truth was, I was scared my breasts would pop out at any moment. Then he asked, "What are you wearing underneath?" The men looked up, like it was a perfectly ordinary question. I felt my cheeks turn red. "Umm, I'm... I'm just wearing my ordinary, umm, panties?"

He turned to the man who liked my feet so much. "Roger, that's a problem. When a girl is dressed as a Princess, there should be nothing 'ordinary' about the experience. Every detail should be special. Princess Bree, would you have preferred that we include some special Princess panties?"

Matt smiled up at me. I knew he was thinking about the Princess panties I'd worn for him on our first date. "Umm, yeah, I guess that would be nice. But umm, there really isn't, umm, room for a bra..." I blushed.

The old man stared at my breasts. "No bra? Mind if I take a look?"

I froze. What did he mean? He was taking a look! All the men were watching me. He stood up, not waiting for my response. I felt his hands slide up and squeeze my breasts, looking right in my eyes. I felt flushed. Someone's grandfather was groping me! "Roger, it's pretty tight up here."

Roger stood up, too, and he slid his hand over my breasts, too. I stood still like a good girl, but I couldn't believe this was happening. Two grown men – strangers! – were groping me in front of everyone! Roger nodded, "Yeah, but she's got pretty big tits. What size tits do you have, Princess Bree?"

"I'm... I'm a 32C?" I practically whispered, feeling out of breath. Two men were feeling me up while I was dressed like a fairy-tale princess!

The men argued about whether they should offer the costumes in size variations. "We should be able to accommodate skinny girls with big racks like this girl, or flat-chested girls, or fat chicks, whatever!" But another man insisted that it would increase the product costs dramatically to offer that many size variations. And their marketing research team hadn't heard anything negative about the sizing. "Look, the skinny girls can wear a padded bra and the girls with big tits can wear no bra. Right, Bree?" The old man smiled at me and gave my breasts a squeeze.

I nodded in agreement. I was in a room full of men talking about my breasts. They sat back down and continued arguing. I stood there, not sure what to do, until one man held up his wine glass for me. I took it into the kitchen to refill it, glad to escape and catch my breath. I poured him more wine. I could barely breath, but I was sure Matt would be so proud of me! We were a great team! I knew he'd close this deal. But I felt so dirty. Strangers groping me, even for important business reasons, felt so gross. So why did it turn me on? I could tell I was so wet. I couldn't wait for the men to go so Matt could get me out of this dress. I wanted my confident powerful businessman boyfriend to fuck my brains out!

As the men left, they all shook hands with Matt. And, one by one, they said goodbye to me. One took my hand and lifted it to his lips and kissed my gloved hand. Another kissed me on the cheek. At last, the old man smiled at me, "You're a fine piece of ass, Princess." Then he turned to Matt, "I think we've got a deal. Send the agreement to my lawyers and we'll get it signed."

When the door closed, I was sure Matt would sweep me up in his arms and carry me off to his bed. But he excitedly grabbed his phone and started dialing while he turned on his laptop. He covered the handset and said, "Clean up a little, kitten, while I tell my team the good news."

I cleared the glasses and plates and stood in the kitchen, barefoot in my princess dress, and rinsed the dishes and put them in the dishwasher. I heard Matt triumphantly telling everyone that he closed the deal. "Yeah, that fucking perv Roger literally could not take his eyes off her bare feet all night. No seriously! And I thought the old man was going to pop a boner when he felt her tits." I could hear the excitement in his voice, but I couldn't help thinking I was only there as eye candy. Didn't he care about me?

But when I walked out of the kitchen, he hung up the phone and closed his laptop. He sighed contently and looked up at me. "We are a hell of a team! I should put you on payroll!" I smiled proudly. "Come here, kitten. Everyone else got to play with those tits tonight. Isn't it my turn?" I walked over obediently and he wrapped his arms around me and buried his face in my breasts. I could tell he was so excited. He'd just closed a major deal. I could almost feel the testosterone pumping through him. He suddenly looked at me aggressively, so hungry for me.

Celebrating Success

Matt picked me up and carried me to his bedroom. He dropped me on the bed roughly and ripped off his jacket and climbed on top of me. He reached up under my princess dress and tugged my panties off. His finger slid right inside me, "Oh, yeah, kitten, you're ready for me."

He yanked my dress up over my hips and unzipped his pants. I felt him guide his hard cock between my legs. He shoved it inside me. This was not the gentle romantic lovemaking I'd expected. He was a hungry animal and he was going to get what he wanted. I moaned as he started fucking me, pinning me to the bed, driving his cock in and out of me.

He flipped me over, pulling me on top of him. "Yeah, ride me, kitten," and I rocked my little ass back and forth, riding his cock in my princess dress. I felt so wild, so hot. I slid up and down on his cock, feeling it inside me. I felt his hands on my ass under my dress, squeezing tight, using my ass to drive me up and down. Then I felt his finger find my tiny little ass. "Oh!" I yelped when I felt his finger enter my ass. He slid it in and out, fingering my ass. I could see the look on his face. "No..." I started to say, but it was too late.

Matt pulled me off of him and turned me face down on the bed and held me down by the back of my neck. He pulled my dress up from behind, exposing my little bare bottom. I felt his cock, dripping wet from my pussy, against my tiny little hole. I closed my eyes tight. He leaned down and whispered in my ear hungrily, "Just relax, kitten, or this is going to hurt."

He pushed gently, but firmly. At first, it wouldn't go in. It was just too big and I was just too tight. But

Matt wasn't going to be denied. I tried my best to relax, but I gripped the sheets and closed my eyes tight. I yelped when I felt him push the head of his cock inside me. It hurt!

He slowly began to push it deeper inside me, and then slide it back and forth. He encouraged me, whispering, "That sweet little ass feels so good," while he grabbed my hair and held me down. Soon he was fucking me, riding me, his cock buried in my ass. I felt so helpless, pinned down wearing a princess dress while a grown man fucked me in the ass. But it made me so hot. Suddenly I felt that familiar feeling in my pussy. I was having an orgasm! I moaned and squirmed, "Oh yes fuck me!" I begged. He shoved it hard into my ass, fucking me, while I had an incredible orgasm. He yelled, "Oh yes!" and I felt his cum shoot into my ass. I couldn't believe it. I had an orgasm without even touching my little clit. I'd never felt that before. And now I had an ass full of cum.

Matt collapsed on the bed next to me. He was still giddy from winning his deal. "Oh, I needed that, kitten!" he smiled and kissed my cheek. I wanted to be mad at him – he'd used me. He didn't even ask before he fucked me in the ass. He even made me wash the dishes! But I couldn't stay mad at him. He'd just given me an orgasm by fucking me in the ass! I smiled back at him.

Then he sat up and gently rubbed my bare bottom. "From the very first moment I saw you wearing those little yoga shorts at that gas station, I was determined to fuck your perfect little ass. It was just sticking out at me, like it was saying, 'Come fuck me, Matt'!"

I smiled up at him while he rubbed my bottom, "My ass does not talk like that!"

"Was that your first time?" he asked.

I nodded.

"I could tell – you looked so scared!" he laughed. "But I knew you'd like it. You look like a princess but you've got a little whore inside you."

I blushed. Did he just call me a whore? And he let his friends feel me up. This relationship was so confusing. "Matt, about us... are we... like... girlfriend/boyfriend?" I looked up hopefully.

He gave me a little spank. "No time to talk! You'd better get going – I've got to talk to our lawyers tonight and get to the office at 5 am. But I owe you one, kitten." He hopped up out of bed, zipped his pants back up, and headed to his home office.

I slowly took off the princess dress and laid it back on his rumpled bed. I put my little miniskirt and pink top back on and walked out. "Umm, bye?" I called out. "Bye!" he yelled back. Not even a kiss goodbye? I rode the elevator down in shame and anger and confusion. But by the time I got to the car, all I could think about was my first anal experience. Wow, it felt so big and deep when it was up there. It was really uncomfortable. My bottom was sore. But it was so hot.

When I sat in my car, I jumped. My bottom really was sore. He'd really given me a good pounding. But I drove home with a smile on my face.

The Business Plan

Being with Matt made me appreciate the good life.
His condo, his car, and his clothes were so expensive
and so nice. And so was his life! Big business deals
and hot art galleries. I wanted some of that life.
But I couldn't even afford to go to the mall.

I didn't have anything appropriate to wear out with
Matt, especially after he'd seen me in the designer
dress. And I certainly didn't trust him to dress me.
I couldn't keep borrowing Sarah's clothes, or her
sister's clothes, because she'd start to get suspicious.
I needed to buy some new clothes that were more
appropriate to my new life. Sexy clothes. Clothes
that men want to rip off of me. But that was a
problem: clothes were expensive, and I didn't have
any money.

How could I earn money? I'd seen from Matt that sex sells. I certainly wasn't going to sell myself – I was no whore, not even a little bit, no matter what Matt said. But models sold sex. Strippers sold sex. Even restaurant hostesses were dressed up to show off. All of them did it without actually selling themselves. What could I do? I tried to think of my options. I had a few things going for me: lots and lots of high school girls I knew who worshipped me. Maybe I could sell something to them?

But I got an idea from the books the school counselor had given me on bullying. Maybe instead of selling something to all those girls, I could sell the girls! I wasn't going to be a pimp, but I bet a lot of men would love to party with hot young cheerleaders like Matt's friends did. I thought of the way those men loved having me at their business party. As I flipped through the books, it occurred to me that I could use all these tactics – peer pressure, body shaming, slut shaming, and all the rest – to convince the girls to do what I wanted. I read the chapter on "relational aggression" closely: "sneaky and insidious type of bullying that often goes unnoticed by parents and teachers. Sometimes referred to as emotional bullying, relational aggression is a type of social manipulation where teens try to hurt a peer or sacrifice their social standing. Relational bullies often ostracize others from a group, spread rumors, manipulate situations and break confidences. The goal behind a relationally aggressive bully is to increase their own social standing by controlling or bullying another person."

I thought to myself how I could use this to convince girls to work for me – everyone wanted to be popular, and if the most popular girl wanted you to do something, you do it, just like Sarah had given me her sister's dress. I just needed the threat of social ostracization.

I decided I would open a business. We'd cater private parties. I thought about calling it 'Teen Aged Party Service', or TAPS. But I kept going back to what Matt had called me: he called me his kitten. It turned me on when he said it. I would call our business 'The Kittens'. I'd innocently explain to the girls (and their mothers) that we were cute and cuddly. But men would know better. I would build a website with pictures of my kittens dressed like little sluts.

I needed a business plan. I called up the best businessman I knew: Matt. I told him I wanted to start a business and I need his advice. We met up at his place. I walked in and dropped to my knees in front of him and unzipped his pants. I eagerly sucked his cock, my blonde head moving up and down, while I rubbed his big balls. He moaned in excitement, surprised by my aggressiveness.

Soon he bent me over his couch and found I wasn't wearing panties under my skirt. He drilled me from behind. I could tell he was so turned on – he was thrusting into me and grunting lustily. I moaned like a little slut, "Yes, fuck me, give it to me!" He pulled out, turned me around, and shoved it back into my mouth. I felt his hot cum shoot into my mouth and down my throat. I tried to swallow it all but some dribbled down my chin. I wiped it off with the back of my hand, smiling up at Matt.

He sat down, exhausted, his pants around his ankles. "Wow, where did that come from?" he smiled. I smiled, pulled my skirt up, and said, "I need your full attention."

I explained my idea. He scratched his head, "So you want to start a catering business? Do you have any experience?"

"Nope!" I smiled. "But I have an army of hot girls. High school cheerleaders. And they'll do what I tell them."

"Well, OK then," he looked dubious but he opened his laptop and created a spreadsheet. It occurred to me that I had a rich investment banker writing the business plan for my little business just because I'd slept with him. Sex was power!

"Here's the deal: you're going to need your costs in here – that's labor costs, equipment, etc. Over here are your revenues – that's the money you make. You need to make more than your costs. That's called profit. And that profit is all you care about."

I nodded, paying close attention as he walked me through it. Then he showed me an example of a marketing plan. He told me I needed to line up several customers before I started paying anyone. "Marketing," he said, "is the art of illusion." He told me to take lots of pictures of the girls for a website and to write up a bunch of fake testimonials. He'd have his web developer bang out a website overnight. I'd just need to upload the photos and some descriptive text.

Then he paused and looked up from his computer. "You know, it occurs to me: there are men with, uh, special interests. You remember Roger from the other night? The guy has a serious foot fetish. Loves feet. If you could identify girls who could meet certain special interests, well, I know people who might want to hire them."

"Like what?" I batted my big green eyes playfully.

He smiled back, "Well, like a foot fetish. Or dressing up like a girl scout. Or a girl willing to let a guy change her diaper. Pretty much anything."

He outlined a plan: the men would have to hire my service. We'd have certain girls there as caterers to serve drinks, but special girls there to entertain the men. No sex, of course, but a pretty good show.

Matt explained that men could easily hire a stripper or a hooker for a party. But the actual cheerleading squad from a high school? And make them all dress like French maids and serve wine? That's impossible.

"So how do you know all these cheerleaders? Are they from your old high school? Or do you have a little sister?" he winked.

"Nope, I go to school with them."

Matt's jaw dropped. "How old are you?"

I smiled up at him and slid my hand between his legs, rubbing his cock in his pants. "Don't worry, I'm legal. But a lot of the girls I'll get aren't legal, so don't get any ideas."

Cheer-washing

I started expanding cheer practice to five nights a week – Tuesdays and Thursdays, as usual, with our coach, but I added Monday, Wednesday, and Friday as captain-led optional extra training days. Then I made sure Sarah and Lindsay let everyone know that it was only optional if you weren't serious about cheer.

It meant that I couldn't ride home with Jake as often. I'd drive myself to school. And when we were together, I was distracted. I just didn't have time for Jake.

After expanding practice, I added a girls-only study hall, led by the cheer squad. I started to handpick girls from the swim team, cross-country team, and other random hot girls I knew. I told them it was very important for girls to have an opportunity to meet in a safe, girls-only environment. We could support each other.

I spoke to the school counselor and asked her to find us a bigger room to meet in after school. And I asked her to come speak to the girls. The counselor was a middle-aged woman who wore shapeless dresses and smelled like lilacs; I didn't need to hear anything she had to say, but it would make our study hall look official. After she spoke to the girls, I gushed to her in the hallway about how great she was. And I asked her to be our faculty advisor. She was glowing with pride when she left.

After that, it was pretty easy to convince the girls to start a business. When I told them they'd be party hostesses, Kylie piped up immediately about all the celebrities who got paid just to show up at club openings and stuff. "We'll be just like celebrities!" she giggled. That girl would do whatever she was told. She was going to make some man very happy. Almost every girl put her name on our signup sheet. The ones that didn't cried to me that they already had after-school jobs or something but they really, really, really wanted to participate.

I had the cheerleaders set up a photoshoot the next day. Kylie categorized the girls by level of hotness. Each girl would have a headshot, taken by Lindsay, with makeup and hair assistance from Kylie and Sarah. And then we'd have the hotter girls take a full-body picture. I'd pushed for bikinis but ultimately we just asked each girl to bring their hottest outfit. It would look more natural that way, anyway.

The best part was the school counselor actually wrote hall passes for all the girls to skip fourth period and come to the library for the photo shoot. The school was officially sanctioning the Kittens! If they saw the photo of me and Lindsay standing by the racks of books in the school library with our eyes meeting like we were about to kiss while dressed in tiny plaid skirts and midriff-baring tops, they might not be so happy about it.

It was a good thing I was so busy building my business. Matt was out of town and didn't even bother to text me. I hadn't gotten laid in a two weeks. I was a very horny girl.

A Bad Boy

As I was walking out of cheer study hall, I saw Finn walking out of detention. He was wearing a dirty black tshirt under a jean jacket and some ripped jeans. His dark hair was messy. He looked like he didn't give a fuck about anything. He looked... hot. I smiled cutely at him, "Oh, hi, Finn. How's detention?"

"Last day," he muttered, walking away.

I saw his strong butt in his jeans. So hot. I couldn't help myself.

"Still mad at me?" I smiled playfully, biting my pouty lip and playing with my ponytail. I was wearing a boring baby blue button-down shirt, but it was unbuttoned low, and I had a short khaki miniskirt that showed off my long tan legs.

"Shut up, Bree," he snarled, assuming I was messing with him, "or I'll give you something to cry rape about." He was so angry. A boy like that would break me in half if he got me in bed. And I needed it.

I gave him a kittenish little pout, "How do you know I wouldn't like it?"

His eyes grew wide. I could tell he didn't trust me – how could he? – but his dick was doing the thinking now. The hottest cheerleader in school was flirting with him? I smiled over my shoulder as I walked away and mouthed, "Come on!" He followed me out to the parking lot without a word and got into my car next to me. He had been planning to take the bus home. He looked in the back seat, "This could work," and looked back at my hot little body.

"No, Finn, I'm not one of those skanks you hang out with."

"OK... want to go to my house? No one's home. Or, we could borrow my brother Brett's place. I hear you like it." He smiled, taunting me.

"No, that place is a dump. I want you to fuck me somewhere slightly cleaner than the men's bathroom in a truckstop."

I could tell by the look on his face that he couldn't believe this was really happening. Was he really going to fuck the high school's hottest cheerleader? He didn't trust me. He looked a little nervous. He hadn't even looked nervous in the principal's office. I loved this power over him.

"Well, my house is OK, then," he smiled and put his hand on my leg, testing me. I let him touch me. It gave me a little thrill to feel his hand on my leg. One of the bad boys was feeling me up.

I drove to his house. He unlocked the door and led me up to his room. It was a dump. Clothes and stuff everywhere. He pushed everything off his bed and smiled, "There. Clean."

I stood in the doorway and smiled seductively. "Finn, you know I'm not some little virgin. I like it wild. Would you mind if I tie you up?" I smiled like a little slut.

I could tell he was conflicted; his brain was telling him not to trust the girl who threatened to get him arrested and had her boyfriend beat him up. But his dick was telling him to shut the fuck up and nail this hot girl. And dicks always beat brains.

He stripped to his boxers while I watched and I tied his wrists securely to the bed, and then his ankles. He was tied down, his big strong body helpless, just wearing baggy boxers. I crawled up on the bed seductively and straddled him. I slowly unbuttoned my shirt, opening it so he could see my little pink bra. I slid my shirt off completely, and then reached back and took off my bra. His eyes locked hungrily on my perky young breasts.

I slid my hands over his strong chest. So firm and smooth. I pinched his nipple and smiled. I could feel his cock growing in his boxers. I slid up and down a little, grinding against him.

"Oh, yeah, baby, fuck me!" he barked. Not very patient of him. I'd have to teach him patience. I slowly kissed his chest, his neck, and back down to his belly. I lifted the waistband of his boxers and peeked in.

"Oh, Finn, I like you already!" I smiled. I reached in and pulled out his big hard cock. It was enormous.

I stroked it gently. "Finn, do you want to fuck me with your big cock?" I smiled cutely.

"Come on, Bree, I want to feel that pussy."

I stroked his cock thoughtfully. I'd never had a man's body under my control before. I tugged his boxers down to his knees. I had a naked man tied to a bed. He was so beautiful with his hard smooth chest, flat abs, and big cock standing straight up. That cock was just delicious! I liked the way it felt in my hand, so firm and throbbing. I liked the shape of it. Even the smell of his cock drove me wild. And I could feel the desire building in him.

"Finn?" I smiled kittenishly up at him, his cock against my soft lips. "Do you like anal?"

"Damn, Bree, you are a freak!" he smiled, "Yeah, I like anal!" I could see his eyes widen, thinking about shoving his big cock into my tight little cheerleader's ass. But that's not what I had in mind.

"Be right back!" I giggled and hopped off the bed. I went to the kitchen and dug around until I found exactly what I needed. Finn started struggling against the ropes when he saw what I was carrying. I worried that the ropes wouldn't hold him – I tied tight knots, but that bed didn't look like it would last if he really started fighting.

I crawled back on the bed and held up giant cucumber with a smile. "This is about the same size as you," I giggled and slid it into my mouth. He watched me take the cucumber in my mouth and he relaxed. I pulled it out and started stroking his cock again, getting him nice and hard. And then I poured some oil on the cucumber until it was slippery.

I slowly took my skirt off for him, revealing my little pink panties. I slid my hand down and gently stroked my silky panties while he watched. Silk felt so erotic against my smooth skin. I felt so free with him tied to the bed. I slid my hands over my body, my eyes meeting his.

I stood up on the bed above him and slowly slid my panties down my long legs while he watched me unveil my shaved pussy. I rubbed the oily cucumber between my legs, closing my eyes and moaning. I smiled like a little tease, my pussy above his big cock pointing straight up at me.

I got down between his legs and kissed his inner thighs gently. My hand found his big balls and gently rubbed, and I pressed his cock against my lips. I inhaled the smell of it and tasted it against my lips. It was such a revelation to have a cock in my hands and at my command. He was moaning already, desperate to feel my warm wet mouth wrapped around his cock.

I slowly slid the tip of his cock between my lips while I looked up at him, my eyes meeting his. I rubbed his balls while I gently sucked on his cock. I felt his whole body tense, his body arching, trying to push deeper into my mouth.

It was then that he felt my finger touch his ass.

"Oh!" his eyes widened and he squirmed. "Whoa whoa whoa…"

I pulled his cock out of my mouth and leaned up, my bare breasts on his hard chest, and I whispered in his ear, "Just relax, kitten, or this is going to hurt." He didn't fight as I lined the cucumber up against his ass. I pushed it in; I had to be firm with him. I wrapped my mouth around his cock, sucking and licking his big cock while I fucked him with the cucumber. He moaned softly, "Yeah, suck it, Bree, suck it, suck it."

I tasted his cock, taking it deeper in my mouth. I was getting better at sucking; with more practice, I'd be a good little cocksucker. Finn's cock was perfect for practice; it was really big, but with him tied up I could control how fast and how deep it went. I tried going fast, and I tried going deep. I felt it in my throat and I was proud I didn't gag. Finn was groaning and squirming under me. All the while, I fucked him with the cucumber, giving it to him fast and deep, too.

I couldn't take it anymore – feeling his body bucking uncontrollably and tasting that big juicy cock made me need him. I pulled the cucumber out and climbed on top. He watched my naked body as I lined up his big cock and slowly slid it into my pussy.

"Oh hell yeah!" he groaned, feeling my tight pussy give way to his big cock.

I rode him like a little cowgirl, grinding up and down, my breasts bouncing with every stroke. I couldn't help moaning; his cock felt incredible inside me. "Don't cum yet!" I ordered while I rode his cock. I fingered my clit while I bounced up and down on his cock. I was so close to orgasm.

Suddenly we both came at the same time, his big cock spurting cum inside me while I writhed in passion. "Oh yes yes yes!" I moaned. "Ohhh!" he yelled in his deep manly voice. I collapsed on his firm chest, our naked bodies pressed together, and put my little blonde head on his chest. His cock was still deep inside me.

I smiled up at him and ran my fingers through his dark wavy hair. He smiled back, triumphant. He'd just nailed the head cheerleader.

"Let me guess: if I tell anyone about this, you'll cry rape?" he teased.

"Nope. You can tell everyone you had anal sex with me," I teased back. For some reason, I was sure he wasn't going to tell anyone. He didn't need to – he had no desire to impress anyone. It made me wonder why he'd texted the picture of me in the first place. I snuggled against his warm body for a moment.

I got up, feeling his cock slide out of me, and gathered up my clothes. He looked a little worried as I put on my bra. "Hey Bree, any chance you could untie me, or do I have to chew my way out of these ropes?"

I ran my hand over his chest. "I like having you tied up!" I smiled. "And I'm a little afraid of what you'll do to me if I untie you," I said as I waved the cucumber and stepped into my skirt.

Finn smiled and tugged at his ropes. "I'm going to slice that thing up and feed it to you."

I gave him a pouty look. "Come on, don't you think I've swallowed enough?" I untied his feet. I leaned over him to untie one of his wrists, pressing my breasts in his face. He relaxed, "Ahh, that's better."

He sat up and rubbed his wrists. I eyed him, wondering what he would do. "So, are we going steady now or what?" he joked.

I rubbed his head, "You're my fuck-toy!" I smiled. I smiled to myself as I drove home. He was so hot, and he was all mine.

A Business Girl

That week I put my plan into action. Lindsay had over 3,000 photos of the twenty-eight girls who'd signed up. She and Kylie picked the best ones. I don't know how they did it, but they had those girls lying on the floor in tiny skirts pretending to do their homework; one girl was looking back over he shoulder with her pencil in her mouth. It was pure sex.

Sarah convinced two of the school's best computer nerds to upload the photos to our website in return for getting to keep a couple private photos for themselves. I personally wrote all the marketing material, trying my best to make it sound innocent and sexy at the same time. It wasn't easy to build a website that a girl's mom would be proud of – and would make men hot. At the end, I was pretty happy. Our business, 'The Kittens' party service, was launched.

The website tracked the hits, and I was shocked how much traffic we were getting. Every girl posted the link to every social media site they knew, and teenage girls posing for the camera was serious click bait. Now if we could just turn some of those clicks into bookings.

Sarah volunteered to train the girls on party service. She taught them how to serve drinks, set tables, and clean up. That girl was really ambitious and aggressive. She reminded me of a younger me!

Building a Business

I wasn't just sitting back waiting for customers to find us. I ordered each of the girls to ask their parents to find us a client. I told them that whoever delivered the first client would be featured on our website and would be honorary cheer captain for a week. I totally invented the 'honorary cheer captain' position; even the girls who weren't on the cheer squad wanted the chance to wear the uniform.

I knew I could get us a party immediately from Matt and his friends, but I didn't dare. If the girls' first working experience was with creepy old men who wanted to dress them up like barefoot princesses and grope them, I'd lose them all. But if they made a little money working hard serving drinks, it wouldn't be that hard to convince them to make a lot of money just looking good for men.

In less than three weeks, we had parties scheduled every weekend for the next three months. Most of the girls had convinced their parents to book a party. Sarah trained the girls on how to serve drinks and food, but mostly they were eye candy. I gave them body-contouring little black dresses and six-inch black heels. I gave them lessons on hair and makeup. They might be terrible at catering, but they looked hot. Very hot.

I worked it out where each party would be staffed by five girls. They'd work for five hours. Each girl would get $10 an hour, or $50 per party. Of course, I charged $20 an hour per girl, so each party cost $500. The fathers of the girls all choked on the cost, but their mothers insisted it showed great initiative and would look great on a college application – I made sure to tell the moms that each girl was an entrepreneur and a part-owner of the business. So for every party, I got $250. And I didn't even have to go.

Each party had a manager, which we called a cheer captain. I tried to pick a girl that would at least show up on time. The cheer captain's job was to suck up to the mom and tell her how great her daughter was. I gave them a little script to memorize. But I didn't forget about the dads. I always made sure their own daughter was never staffed to work her own family's party. And I picked another girl to flirt with the dad. Make him feel special. Sarah was the best at it. The girl was talented. At the end of every party, no matter how badly they'd bungled the service or how many plates they'd broken, I always got paid. And the girls got big fat tips from the fathers.

Sarah was a bit of a concern, though. Some of the girls complained that she would make sure she got the biggest tip from the fathers. And she was a bully at the parties, even pushing around the 'cheer captain'. I'd have to talk to that girl. But she was bringing in the cash.

I was so busy launching the business that I forgot all about Matt. But I couldn't forget my urges. I'd wake up in the morning needing a man. By the end of the school day, I was so hot and wet that I would have dropped my panties for the janitor if he spoke enough English to ask me. I would text Finn in last period and tell him to meet me at his house. I had 45 minutes between the final bell and the start of cheer practice. I couldn't be late. With Finn, I didn't have to be. He'd happily be handcuffed to his bed so I could go for a quick ride before practice. Finn was happy, I thought; he was nailing me regularly, even if he did have to take the occasional spanking or anal rape from me. And I was getting fucked, so I was happy.

I noticed my dreams had changed. Instead of dreaming about Matt or Brett, I dreamt about Finn. Finn's big cock. Finn's hard body. Finn licking my clit while tied to the bed. But I dismissed the dreams. He was just my fuck-toy. Nothing emotional about it.

A month after we started, my bank account exploded. I had the dads pay me directly online, and with four or five parties every weekend, the cash was rolling in. I checked my bank balance more often than my text messages. I decided to ask the dads to send the tips to me, too, rather than giving them directly to the girls. I told the girls about it after one of them complained that the dad didn't have any cash so they only got a $5 tip, so they believed it was just a way to get bigger tips. But the reality is that it gave me even more control, especially over Sarah, who had gotten worse and worse. She would collect all the tips and pay the girls based on who she thought deserved the most. The girls had to suck up to her as much as me! But now they wouldn't know how big the tips were until I paid them, and Sarah wouldn't have control over them. And I'd get my share, too. Which, of course, I deserved.

Homecoming

I'd entirely forgotten about Homecoming. It was a big game and, despite our five-day-a-week practices, the cheer squad wasn't ready. We spent a lot of practice time working on our business, not our cheers. Sarah had a solution: sluttier uniforms. Our regular uniforms were skimpy, but she found some online that were really hot. They had tiny skirts and tops that were little more than bras. And we'd wear knee-high white boots. I knew it didn't matter how we cheered if we walked out like that. But the uniforms were expensive and Ms. Simpson was never going to go for it. So I decided to use business funds to buy the uniforms; I could have the girls wear them to parties, too. I'm sure they'd be very popular.

On the Tuesday before Homecoming, the student body voted for the Homecoming Court. I didn't do any of my normal politicking; I was just too busy. I'd even ignored three texts from Matt. I hoped I'd done enough for Sarah to at least finish a respectable third in the princess voting. After school I immediately went to Finn's house. I loved it that his mom had to work so much. We always had an empty house to use.

Finn was waiting for me, but not in the bedroom. He was sitting in the kitchen.

I dangled the handcuffs. "Come on, sweetheart," I smiled.

He frowned. "Bree, we need to talk."

"No, we don't need to talk. We need to fuck. That's what we do."

"That's what we need to talk about."

I sighed and sat down. Our eyes met. He sighed, too, and told me a story.

"Remember when we were in the principal's office? And I said I'd always loved you?"

I nodded, hoping he'd hurry this along. I had stuff to do. I had to get the girls fitted for their new uniforms and I needed a new Homecoming queen dress.

"Well, it was true. I've had a crush on you since 3rd grade, Bree. And when this... whatever this is... starting happening, I was really happy. But I was kinda hoping, that, you know, maybe sometime we could actually go out? Or just talk?"

I smiled at him seductively, "So you don't want to fuck me?"

"Of course I want to fuck you. Everyone wants to fuck you. But I want more than that."

I sat there quietly playing with an envelope sitting on the kitchen counter. It was from our school. I knew what it was, because there was one sitting in my house, too: mid-term report cards. I had a sinking feeling. I'd been so busy that I was sure my grades were slipping. I looked up and his eyes were locked on mine.

"Don't be such a chick, Finn."

He got up and walked out. Fucking drama queen. I sighed. It shouldn't be this hard to get laid. I absent-mindedly opened the envelope and read his report card. Finn got straight As? What the fuck was this? And he was taking AP History and AP English? I was expecting Cs in woodshop or something, if the school had a class in woodshop. It occurred to me that I really didn't know much about the boy I was fucking.

I spent that evening simultaneously dealing with crybaby girls and their uniform fitting issues and trying to juggle four different party reservations for Homecoming weekend. All the girls wanted to go to the Homecoming dance, which left me with no one to staff a party at the same time. I never should have taken the reservation, but they offered to pay double. I couldn't resist. But the girls didn't want to do it, even for $20 an hour. But I couldn't stop thinking about Finn. There was more to him than I'd known.

Outfoxed

Wednesday was a complete disaster. Because I was on Student Council, I helped count the votes for the Homecoming Court. My stomach dropped when I realized what was happening: Sarah was winning. That little skank must have been politicking behind my back. She wasn't just going to defeat Lindsay and Kylie for princess, she was going to steal my crown! Sarah, a sophomore, crowned Homecoming Queen?

It didn't take long to see that she was winning in a landslide. While I was building the business and riding Finn's cock, Sarah was winning votes. But the queen's tiara wasn't all she stole from me; while we were counting votes, Jake could barely meet my eyes. After we'd finished counting and I'd ended up in second place – distant second – Jake asked to talk to me. I assumed he was going to try to make me feel better about losing. I was wrong.

"Bree, it's just, you've barely had time for me for the last couple of months, and I, well, I mean, Sarah thinks, that it would be nice if the King and Queen went to Homecoming together..."

I put it together quickly. Sarah, that two-faced little bitch, stole my tiara -- and my boyfriend? It didn't matter that I'd matured so much recently that I didn't really care about either one. It was the principal of the matter. You don't steal from me. I needed to teach the little skank a lesson.

The Homecoming Court votes were tallied, and Sarah was Queen. I was one Princess and Kylie as the other. That left Lindsay out. Jake was elected King, as expected. There was no way I was going up on stage as one of Sarah's Princesses while she was on Jake's arm. So I went to Lindsay in tears.

"It's just not fair that Sarah got you kicked off the Homecoming court!" I cried. Lindsay was stunned. She was beautiful, if a little dumb, and was used to getting what she wanted. How could she have lost? I saw the tears welling up in her eyes. But I told her my plan: I'd step down from the Homecoming court so Lindsay could be a Princess.

Lindsay looked at me, stunned, both of us crying. "You'd do that for me?"

I nodded and she hugged me. She cried, "You're always so sweet to me, Bree. It's just not fair!"

Then I told her that Sarah had cheated. I told her how Sarah also stole my boyfriend. I told her Sarah won by only one vote, and Jake had been the one counting them.

"I wish there was something we could do!" Lindsay cried. "I always thought Sarah was nice, but now..."

I rubbed Lindsay's back and told her, "We'll think of something. We can't let her get away with this! We're supposed to be cheer sisters!"

Lindsay nodded, wiping her tears, "I'll help you!"

I was counting on it.

Next I called Matt and told him I was ready to have my girls work a party for him.

"I've missed you, kitten!" he said confidently. I could hear his smile over the phone. So masculine, so mature. I was instantly wet. I'd only slept with Finn in the past month or so, and I'd never really thought of Matt much, but hearing his voice made me purr.

Matt set up a party with his clients from the costume manufacturer and his buddies from work. He wanted ten girls; I told him it would cost $10,000. He just laughed. He laughed! He told me they'd just been in Vegas and four of them had gotten table service at a club. They'd blown $20,000 in one night. He was happy to pay $10,000.

"I've always been a big supporter of small businesses," he laughed.

Finally, I drove over to Finn's house. It was seven o'clock at night and the lights were on and there was a car in the driveway. I rang the doorbell and a woman answered.

"Hello?" she looked at me in a friendly, if tired, way.

"Hi, I'm Bree, is Finn home?"

"Bree?" She smiled. "The Bree?"

She invited me in and called to Finn. He came out of his room wearing camo cargo shorts and a black wife-beater. I was wearing sandals, little white shorts, and a white polo shirt with my hair up in a blonde ponytail. We couldn't have looked more different. I smiled at him. He was so cute. He looked back at me, confused at why I was here.

His mom excused herself and we sat down at the kitchen table. "Do you own any clothes better than those?" I nodded toward his outfit.

He smiled, "I've got some jeans, too."

"I'm thinking of a jacket and tie."

"Why? Am I wanted in court?" he looked at me with skepticism and a tiny bit of hopefulness.

"Well, there's a school dance this weekend and I need a date..."

Finn jumped up and hugged me tight, then let me go.

"Sorry, sorry!" he smiled.

A Change of Uniforms

In class on the Friday of Homecoming weekend, I looked down at my phone under my desk. My phone was blowing up with messages. I had girls whining about having to work parties on homecoming weekend, clients requesting specific girls, girls whining about the way their Kittens dresses fit, and my cheer coach asking suspicious questions about our new uniforms. We were wearing our regular uniforms to school; I'd planned the big unveil of the new uniforms for the football game. I looked up at saw our Social Studies teacher start to write 'quiz' on the whiteboard. I had done no studying; I needed to buy some time. I turned to the boy next to me, a guy named Tyler that I'd known since kindergarten.

I whispered, "Tyler, can you buy me some time?" There were 15 minutes left in class. I had to run out the clock before the quiz, and I needed to send some messages in the meantime.

Tyler knew exactly what to do. "Mr. Jones? My uncle is like a hard-core Republican, and he says the government spends too much money?"

Mr. Jones' pen froze on the whiteboard, his hand dotting the i in 'quiz'. He turned to the class, pushing up his glasses. Mr. Jones was a loyal Democrat and took his responsibility to indoctrinate students into party doctrine very seriously.

"Well," Mr. Jones chuckled, getting warmed up.

Another kid knew the game and chimed in immediately – he obviously didn't want to take the quiz either. "Yeah, I heard the government steals most of the money anyway..."

Like a lawnmower, sometimes it took a pull or two to get Mr. Jones started. But I could see his hand trembling as he held his pen.

"Well, well, do you think you can spend too much on safe drinking water? Hmm? What about medicine for poor sick children? Yes?"

He pushed his glasses up and then seemed to change his mind and take them off, knocking them off his face and sending them tumbling to the ground. But his rant was started and he wasn't going to be stopped. He continued talking while he bent over and retrieved his glasses. Eye rolls rippled around the classroom.

"One Party wants you to grow up safe and protected, with good schools, with a clean environment, and allow you to make your own choices about your bodies, and the other doesn't," he rambled.

Tyler interrupted, "But not choices about schools, right? The Party is against school choice, right?"

I happened to know that Tyler was an Anarcho-Socialist, not a Republican, but everyone loved fucking with the teachers.

"School choice? School choice? You know what that really means? That means stripping teachers like me of our rights... " Mr. Jones' face was red and he waved his glasses in the air to punctuate his rant. I put my phone in my lap and typed away. There would be no quiz today. He was still talking when the bell rang and we all filed out.

"I owe you one, Ty," I winked.

"Yeah, find me a date for Homecoming then," he smiled back at me as he pulled on his backpack and trudged down the hall.

At the Homecoming game, our football team absolutely demolished our cross-town rivals. But not many people noticed because our cheer squad was dressed like hookers. Our cheer routines weren't particularly new or well executed, but because we performed them dressed in tiny little slut-wear, the crowd roared their approval. Sarah was so proud of herself, little miss Homecoming Queen, and she cheered her heart out.

At halftime she had to make a quick change, along with Lindsay and Kylie, into their dresses and sashes, and walk out to midfield. It was a change I'd made before; strangely, even though I was committed to revenge, I didn't really care too much about missing out. I didn't care as much about what the school thought of me anymore.

After halftime I noticed the rival quarterback watching Sarah proudly shaking her ass just before he got sacked. The school really owed us for this

one!

Our First Date

Finn drove up to my house in his mom's car. My mom was shocked to learn that I wasn't going with Jake. She'd called around to the other moms, but none of them knew much about Finn. The little they did know gave my mom a scare. "So this boy is in trouble a lot?" she asked while I did my hair.

"Mom!" I ordered her out. I'd gotten myself a new outfit, paid for by the Kittens, and it was just for Finn. She wasn't going to like it, so it was best she only saw me on my way out the door. And I didn't have much time between the game and the dance to get ready.

I heard Finn downstairs introducing himself to my dad. I let him sweat a little, and then I walked down the stairs. I was wearing a fire engine red dress, and it was tight in all the right places. My blonde hair was up and I had fishnet thigh-highs – my new favorite – and sky-high heels. This was not a high school girl's dress. I was definitely going to stand out in the crowd. But I found myself most excited about what Finn thought of it.

My dad and Finn turned when they heard me coming down the stairs. My mom put her hand over her mouth when she saw my dress. But I couldn't pay any attention to her. Finn looked hot! He was wearing a white dinner jack, cut very narrow, that accentuated his muscular body. He had on a white shirt and a black bow tie. He looked so elegant! I smiled at him and he smiled back. When I got to the bottom of the stairs, he handed me a bouquet of roses. I blushed! I gave them to my mom so she could put them in a vase for me.

Before he led me out, my mom whispered to me, "I can't say I approve of the dress, but the boy is very cute!" I smiled proudly and walked out to Finn's car. He opened the door for me like a gentleman.

Before he even turned the car on, I turned to Finn and said, "So you're a straight A student? And you take AP classes?"

He looked at me and laughed. "Why? Do I look stupid to you?" Then he smiled softly. "I don't really give a damn what the school thinks of me. But I care what you think."

I sat there quietly, my hands in my lap. "I care what you think, too."

We drove over in silence, but not uncomfortable silence. I wasn't trying to think of something to say, I just enjoyed being with him. When he reached over to take my hand, it seemed like the most natural thing in the world to hold hands with him.

When we got to the school, he parked well away from the doors and we sat in the dark. "I'm going to do something we've never done before," he said, and leaned over and kissed me. Our mouths met and he gently, but passionately, kissed me. And I kissed him back. I smiled as he led me in to the school. I'd never kissed him when I'd met him at his house. I don't know why. I'd expected him to taste like cigarettes, even though I'd never seen him smoke. He just had that reputation. But he didn't. He tasted like mint.

Finn stopped me at the door to the school gym and he put his hands on my shoulders, our eyes meeting. "Bree, for tonight, I am the man in this relationship..."

"If you have to say that, then you probably aren't," I smiled.

"I'm just saying I would prefer it if you didn't sodomize me over the punch bowl."

I smiled up at him. "Don't worry! I'll try to act respectable in front of your high-class friends!"

I couldn't help laughing. My burnout boyfriend was worried about my behavior. He thought I'd embarrass him. Suddenly it occurred to me that I'd just thought of Finn as my boyfriend. Finn saw me smiling and smiled back.

Before he opened the door to the gym, he turned to me again.

"I just wish we'd had a practice date before we did it in front of the whole school," he said.

I could tell he was nervous. It was cute. He was nervous on our first date! I smiled up at him and said, "Would it help if I told you that you're going to get lucky tonight, and there won't be any handcuffs? You're the man?"

He smiled back at me and put his hand on my back, guiding me in as he opened the door. He whispered, "You know, we could skip the dance and go straight to that part." I walked in, smiling. I knew the whole place was going to skip a beat when they saw the boy who walked me in – but I was happy!

Sarah's Victory Dance

The crowd parted when we entered. It wasn't just who we were – Bree and Finn, together. It wasn't just the shock of me with someone other than Jake, or not being on the Homecoming Court. It was because together, we looked really hot. We looked like a celebrity couple. Finn had his hand confidently and possessively on my back. He guided me through the crowd, ignoring everyone. He only had eyes for me.

Lindsay, Kelsey, and Kylie appeared immediately. They ran up excitedly and then didn't say anything, shocked and confused, in front of Finn. Finn smiled at me, "Can I get you something to drink?"

I nodded and he walked off, leaving me with the girls. The girls watched him go and then exploded.

"Ohmygod Bree!" gushed Kylie, "Jake is going to be sooo jealous!"

"I didn't know he was so... so... so hot!" smiled Lindsay as he walked away.

"Bree, it's like a movie where you take a total social leper and transform him!" giggled Kelsey.

"I didn't transform anyone," I laughed. "Finn just really doesn't give a damn what the school thinks of him." The truth was, I didn't care that much either. "He's just dressed like that for me."

They went on and on about what a backstabbing bitch Sarah was, and how Jake had totally betrayed me. I tried to pay attention but I couldn't help looking across the gym to see where Finn had gone. He was talking to some other girls. I was jealous! I saw him talking to other girls and it made me jealous.

How dare they talk to my boyfriend? I smiled to myself. The girls all looked at me.

"What?" I said, not following the conversation.

"What are we going to do about Sarah and Jake?" Lindsay demanded. She owed me and she knew it. And she was determined to pay me back. But I just shrugged.

"Just enjoy your night, Lindsay," I smiled, "We'll figure that out later." The wheels were already in motion.

I yawned through the Homecoming court ceremony. I couldn't believe I used to take this so seriously. Jake looked pretty nervous up there with Sarah. But Sarah looked radiant. 'Enjoy your moment of triumph, Sarah', I thought to myself. It wouldn't last.

I felt Finn next to me before I saw him. Our eyes met. "Wish you were up there?" he asked gently.

"Nope," I smiled and changed the subject, "Hey, did you quit smoking?"

He paused, and then said, "Well, I noticed you never kissed me during our... our rendezvous. So I quit."

I leaned up and kissed him on his cheek.

Halfway through our second dance, with Finn holding me close, I whispered in his ear, "Want to take me out of here?" He smiled down at me and we kissed, right there on the dance floor in front of everyone. And he took my hand and led me out.

In the backseat of his mom's car, Finn pulled my dress up and I pulled his pants down. The car was rocking when Finn climbed on top of me. I put my arms around his neck and we kissed as he penetrated me.

That night, for the first time, we made love. When he collapsed on top of me, panting and grinning, I could tell he loved me. And I was pretty sure he could tell the feeling was mutual.

"Wow, my first time on top!" he smiled.

"Yeah, don't get too used to it, buddy," I laughed, "I like dominating you!"

I reached down and gently stroked his cock until he got hard again. This time, he used his fingers to rub my clitoris while he fucked me, making sure I had an orgasm before he did. We collapsed together, the windows fogged up.

We went back into the dance, not caring that my hair was messy and his jacket was wrinkled. We danced together, his eyes sparkling as he looked at me.

I joined the girls again briefly while Finn talked to some guys. The girls surrounded Sarah while she stood in the middle and basked in their attention. I heard her talking about the Kittens – my business! –

as if she ran it. "We need black girls, you know, to broaden our appeal," she said. The Kittens had two Asian girls and three Hispanic girls, but otherwise was mostly white. Lindsay reminded her that we had Brittany, one of our cheerleaders.

"Well, she's only half-black," Sarah interrupted.

"I think she's like a quarter black or something. But all her whiteness went to her ass. We need black girls with those big ghetto booties. Guys love those!" Kylie said.

I stood there and steamed. This was my business and I would decide how many black booties or Asian girls we had. Who the hell did Sarah think she was? She stood there with her stupid tiara on her head, smiling so proudly.

I was going to get her.

Baiting the Trap

"She's a virgin, Matt," I said, baiting him, "I don't think she can do it." I took a spoonful of yogurt.

His ears perked up. A virgin? I could tell the idea thrilled him and I could see the wheels turning in his head. I'd always wondered what the fascination was with virgins. When I was a virgin, I just lay there and took it. But now I could suck and fuck just like a little sex addict. Why would you want a virgin over a girl like me?

"What's the big deal with virgins?" I sighed, licking my spoon.

Matt explained, "See your yogurt? Let's say I give you a choice between two yogurts. One is brand-new, unopened, fresh cherry yogurt. The other one has already been opened and I stuck my dick in it. Which one do you want?"

I laughed.

We got to work; we had a $10,000 party to plan. Matt flipped through the photos of the girls like he was ordering off a menu. He considered dressing them all like princesses, like he'd done to me. But ultimately he decided he wanted black leather bikinis and sky-high black heels. I shook my head, "Seriously, Matt?"

But it was his party and his money, and he paid in advance in cash. I couldn't believe it. Matt handed me five stacks of strapped $20 bills, each strap containing 100 twenty-dollar bills. $10,000 cash in my hand. All crisp, new bills. I'd never held this much money before. I'd never seen this much money before, except in the movies.

While holding the money, I just nodded as Matt walked through our responsibilities at the party.

Each guest would be assigned a girl as his personal hostess. His hostess would escort him throughout the party. I could just imagine the scene: girls in leather bikinis escorting older men, drinking and partying. But the cash felt good in my hands, so I wasn't complaining. I did make one thing clear, though: we weren't prostitutes.

"I'm not having sex with any of your creepy friends, Matt," I said, meeting his eyes bravely. "And my girls aren't either."

"Except one, right?" he asked.

"Yeah, except Sarah," I nodded.

Before I left, Matt had me on my knees to give him a blowjob. I didn't want to have sex with him; I felt like that would be a betrayal of Finn. But oral sex wasn't sex. And besides, it was business. As I felt his hard cock in my mouth, my lips wrapped around it while I sucked, I felt conflicted. I should be sucking Finn's cock. But Matt closed his eyes and grabbed my hair while he shoved his hips into my face, fucking my mouth. I could feel he was ready to explode when he pulled out and tugged on his cock until he shot cum all over my face.

"Nice, Matt," I said as I wiped cum from my cheeks and lips.

"Just reminding you that you work for me now, kitten," he smiled down at me.

I went to his bathroom to wash my face. I saw my face in the mirror sticky with Matt's cum. I thought about Finn. After Homecoming, I'd expected we'd be inseparable, but tonight, a Friday night, he'd said he was busy. Too busy for me? I was stunned. I'd quickly reached out to Matt to do the party planning, but maybe in the back of my mind I'd given Matt a

blowjob to get back at Finn for blowing me off.

A Spa Day

I had all the girls I'd picked for Matt's party meet me
at the spa. I had appointments for all of them;
they'd all get manicures, pedicures, and have their
hair blown out and styled and their makeup done.
I'd hand-picked the girls. Sarah, of course, was
there. I also had Kelsey, Lindsay, and Kylie, three
other cheerleaders who were pretty loyal to me, and
two other hot girls who desperately wanted to be
popular.

I turned to Sarah while we were getting our nails
done and casually asked, "You're not a virgin, are
you?" She blushed, and I could tell by the way she
stammered, "N-n-no" that she was. I knew it; I just
needed to confirm.

"Good!" I smiled. "There will be some older guys at
the party!" I smiled, feigning excitement. Sarah

smiled back nervously. She had to be wondering

what her virginity had to do with older men, but she

didn't dare ask. I knew she didn't want to look like a

little kid in front of the other girls. The other girls

giggled and asked excited questions about the older

men. They all obviously felt so mature, enjoying

their spa treatments before going to work as

professional hostesses.

All of us had shown up on time for a change, and

they were all excited. I'd told them we were starting

a new line of parties, celebrity-style parties, but only

the most mature girls could participate. And they

had to agree to keep it secret.

While the stylist blew out Lindsay's long dark hair

and gave her a little curl at the ends, she told

everyone she hoped she'd meet a rich older

boyfriend at the party. They all giggled with

excitement. Our eyes met and I nodded to Lindsay;

I'd coached her and Kylie. Each girl expected to get $50 an hour for the party, so I'd committed $2,250 to the girls. I'd keep $7,750 for myself. $50 an hour for five hours was a fortune for a girl in our school. We all talked about how we'd spend the money – new clothes, new phones, or new shoes.

Kylie spoke up and told the girls we had to be super hot so these rich men would tip us really well. She turned to Sarah and said, "Sarah, you're so good at getting big tips – you have to help us!"

Sarah beamed at the recognition. This was going to be so easy. I sat back and enjoyed a foot massage while the girls chatted excitedly. When the limo picked us up, they could barely control their excitement. I had to beg them not to take pictures and post them – everyone, including their parents, would know we were up to something if a photo of all of us exiting a spa in a limo hit the social sites.

In the limo, I handed each girl a bag with her bikini and heels and I collected up their phones and keys and stuff. I had to have their phones; I couldn't let anything about this party leak. Kylie and Lindsay, who knew in advance what we would wear, opened their bags excitedly and gushed about how hot the bikinis were. Some of the other girls looked dubious, but didn't dare say anything. I saw the look of shock on Sarah's face. Her tiny bikini would show off every inch of her firm young body and she knew it. But she didn't say a word and even forced a fake smile while the girls around her laughed and held their bikini tops up to their chests.

At Matt's condo, the girls couldn't believe how amazing it was. Matt wasn't there; I'd told him that the girls couldn't know we knew each other. The place was already set up; Matt had arranged food from some caterer and the bar was already stocked.

There was nothing for the girls to do but get dressed. The girls wandered the condo excitedly. "He must be so rich!" gushed Lindsay.

I led them all into Matt's bedroom to get changed. I sat on the bed I'd shared with him while the girls got changed. They laughed excitedly as they saw each other in the bikinis. They pranced around in their heels in front of the mirror, sticking their chests out. I smiled at the girls, "Wow, we are going to blow their minds!"

But when I put my bikini on, I was a little reluctant. My mind kept returning to Finn. I'd expected that I'd have to make excuses not to see him, but before I could say anything he'd told me he was busy again. Almost every weekend, he had a night when he was "busy". What the hell did that mean? We all walked out and wandered nervously around the condo in our bikinis and heels. But I was nervous for a different reason. Was Finn cheating on me?

But I didn't have long to think about it, because we all froze when we heard the key in the door. The door opened and Matt entered, followed by nine other men. The girls, so confident and giggly just a moment before, were standing frozen in their bikinis.

But Matt put them at ease with his confident smile. "Hello, girls! I'm so glad you're here." He explained they were celebrating a huge business deal and were delighted with the beautiful company. Then he asked the girls if they wanted a drink. Matt stood behind the bar and instead of the girls serving him, he served them, offering each one a glass of champagne and a compliment. Watching him win them over made me think how easy it must have been for him to seduce me.

A Grownup Party

Soon the music was pumping and the men were drinking heavily. The girls, dizzy from champagne, were soon dancing and drinking with them. I heard one of the men, an older man in his 30s with a goatee that he probably thought looked cool way back in like 2005 ask Lindsay if he could snort some coke off of her belly. She giggled and agreed. He laid her down on the bar and the men took turns doing lines off her firm cheerleader abs. "Me next! Me next!" giggled Kylie.

I turned to Sarah and smiled, "You should do it!"

She looked nervous. Kelsey whispered, "Come on, Sarah, we need you to get us big tips!" Sarah stepped forward. Soon the men were doing lines from her breasts in the little bikini. And she seemed to like it. The girls were laughing and giggling. The man with the goatee, Eric, lifted his head from between Sarah's breasts, sniffing.

"Come on guys, give the girls a turn!" I laughed. Eric hopped up on the bar and laid back and pulled up his shirt. Not exactly gym-rat abs, but not too bad. "Come on, girls!" he laughed and rubbed cocaine on his belly.

Sarah looked around nervously. Our eyes met and I encouraged her. I'd never done coke before and she obviously hadn't either; tonight was going to be a night of firsts for her. One of the men handed Sarah a straw and she tentatively took a snort from Eric's belly.

Eric cheered and the men roared. The girls all laughed. Soon half the girls were snorting coke with the men and chasing it with champagne. An hour into the party, half the girls were dancing in their heels and bikinis with cocaine-fueled passion, their half-naked bodies dusted with white powder. Matt smiled at me. This was exactly what he wanted.

Eric turned to me and Matt while wiping the cocaine from his nose and nodding toward Sarah. He said, "I love that little girl-next-door look; she's worth every penny of my $20,000!"

I turned to Matt in shock. "What $20,000?"

He just smiled and whispered, "You're a businesswoman, right? You're charging me $10,000 but paying your talent about half of that?"

I nodded. I was paying them about a quarter of that, but Matt didn't need to know it.

Matt took a sip of champagne and continued, "Well, that's the essence of business. Buy low, sell high. You wanted me to pop your little friend's cherry. I sold her virginity for $20,000. I paid you half. That's fair."

"Wait, so, who's going to do it?" I looked up, confused. Somehow it had seemed okay when I asked Matt to do it; at least I knew him. And I didn't ask him to pay to do it! Did I just prostitute out one of my own cheerleaders?

Matt pointed over at Eric. "Eric is the lucky highest bidder."

I shook my head, "I don't know, Matt, she'll never go for it." I looked over at Sarah. Now she was dancing with Eric, his hands on her hips, and she had her back to him, bending over and grinding her little bikini-clad body against him. The dazed look on her face said she was drunk and high. What had I done?

Matt laughed, "Oh, I think she'll do just fine."

I tilted back my glass of champagne and finished it. This was going too far. Sarah had stolen my boyfriend, but I didn't want Jake back. She'd stolen my Homecoming crown, but I wasn't sure I cared about that, either. She was elbowing her way into leadership in my business, but I was the one making all the money and she was the one going to the parties and doing all the work. Why was I punishing her again?

My heart was in my throat when I saw Eric guiding her back to Matt's bedroom. She was drunk and giggling and he had his hands on her hips, walking behind her, whispering something in her ear. The rest of the girls barely noticed. They were dancing on the coffee table, letting men do body shots off of them, and taking selfies with men by the wall-to-ceiling windows. At least they were using the guys' phones; hopefully those photos wouldn't make it back to school. I saw the bedroom door close behind Sarah and Eric. I held my glass out for Matt to pour me more champagne. I needed it.

At about midnight, the party was dying down. Eric had excited the bedroom triumphantly, raising his arms in the air, but he didn't say anything about what he'd done. I was glad the other girls didn't know. He left quietly after saying something to Matt. Roger, the guy who liked my feet when I was dressed as a princess, was sitting on the couch with Kylie and Lindsay. Both of them had their feet in his lap and he was taking turns giving them foot massages. He had a disturbingly excited look on his face.

"Ohhh, that feels so good, Roger," Lindsay cooed, "My heels really hurt my feet."

I rolled my eyes. Roger had a stack of $20 bills next to him and he was handing them individually to each girl. I saw that Kylie had at least $80 tucked into her bikini.

Sarah was sitting by herself on the edge of the couch. Our eyes met. I could see the tears welling up. I went to her and she whispered, "Can we talk? Privately?" Her big sad eyes looked up at me.

I took her back to Matt's bedroom. The covers on his normally immaculate bed were a mess. She started crying immediately.

"What happened, Sarah?" I asked, pretending not to know and feeling guilty.

She poured it out as the tears streamed down her cheeks. She didn't know how it happened; she'd been dancing with him and then they were making out and then they were having sex.

"I'm a virgin!" she cried, "I mean, I was…"

She told me how it all happened so quickly. He pushed her onto the bed and it was like her bikini just melted off.

I hugged her, our bodies pressed together in our bikinis. I really felt bad. I'd done this. I had to get her out of there.

She sobbed, her little body heaving against mine, "I never even took my heels off!" I thought to myself that I never took my heels off my first time, either.

"Come on, Sarah, let's get dressed and go." I went out and told Matt the party was over; he'd paid for five hours and we'd given him four, but I thought it was fair. I rounded up the girls, still giggly and drunk and high, and herded them back to the bedroom. The remaining men reluctantly left.

Once we were dressed and walked out of the bedroom, only Matt remained. He sat on the couch sipping on bourbon. He stood when we filed out.

"Girls, that was fantastic. You rock!" he smiled. He pulled an envelope out of his pocket and held it out to Sarah. "The guys left some money as a tip."

She didn't dare meet his eyes when she took the envelope, and she didn't open it immediately. Once we were back in the limo, the girls were dying to see how much money we'd gotten as a tip. When Sarah opened the envelope, the thick stack of crisp bills caused a collective gasp. It was almost $2,000, or $200 for each girl. On top of the $250 I was paying each of them, that was $450 each for four hours of work. Lindsay and Kylie made even more from their little foot party with Roger. The girls were ecstatic. Everyone except Sarah.

Betrayal

In the limo, I gave the girls their phones back. My phone had a ton of text messages, but nothing from Finn. One of them, however, was from a girl named Rose who came to our empowerment study hall – I'd changed the name to 'Empowerment Study Hall' at the suggestion of the school counselor who couldn't stop forwarding me articles from various women's studies departments in colleges around the country. Rose had sent me a photo of Finn walking with another girl. I couldn't believe it. She wasn't even hot – she was dressed in all black with ripped up fishnets. How could he do this? How could he cheat on me? I thought he loved me. This must be what he's been doing when he was "too busy" for me almost every weekend.

Sarah saw the look on my face, but she assumed I still felt bad for her. She put her head on my shoulder. I stroked her hair gently. We both got screwed that night.

I went home and crawled into bed, but I couldn't sleep. I just tossed and turned. What had I become? I used to be the most popular girl at school. Now I was pimping out my friends and my boyfriend was cheating on me. I didn't know what hurt more. I thought over what I would say to Finn. I got my phone out a bunch of times through the night, but the words never came to me.

The next morning I had a text message from Finn: "We need to talk."

This was it. He was going to break up with me. Tears rolled down my cheeks. I called Sarah; it was all I could think to do.

"How are you doing?" I asked.

She paused, but said she was OK. I listened to her describe what happened, now that she was sober. I wanted to tell her that it was all my fault, but I didn't dare. Instead I told her about Rose's photo and about Finn's text message.

She was so sympathetic. She actually sounded like she felt worse for me than I did for her, and she didn't do anything to me. It just made me feel worse. She arrived at my house in twenty minutes with coffee. We sat at the kitchen table nursing hangovers.

"So what are you going to do?" she asked.

I sighed. "I guess I'm going to see him. I... I deserve it anyway."

"But that bastard is the one cheating! He deserves to get his ass kicked!" she complained.

"No, I'm not into revenge anymore. I'm not any good at it," I said as I put my head on the table. Sarah rubbed my back.

I walked into Finn's house and sat at the kitchen table opposite him. He looked across the table at me and asked, "What did you do to Sarah?"

"Sarah?" I looked up at him in confusion. "What does this have to do with Sarah?" Had she stolen another boyfriend of mine?

Finn explained that Jake had come to see him last night. Apparently Sarah called Jake and told him everything: she'd lost her virginity to some stranger while drunk at a party. A party that I had arranged. She was convinced Jake would dump her, but she couldn't lie to him. Jake had gone to Finn – he wanted Finn to ask me what to do. Now Jake was asking Finn for advice? The world was spinning out of control.

"Wait, so, when you texted me that 'we need to talk', it was about Sarah?"

"Well, yeah, what else would it be?"

"I thought you were breaking up with me," I said, tears forming.

"Why would I break up with you?" he asked in genuine bewilderment. I handed him my phone and showed him the picture Rose had sent me.

Finn laughed. "That's my bass player. Believe me, she'd like you more than she likes me."

"Your bass player? What are you talking about?"

Finn explained that he was in a band. They'd been playing anywhere that would let them, which is why he hadn't had a lot of time to spend with me on weekends recently.

"But why wouldn't you tell me you're in a band?" I cried.

"Because we suck," he explained. He told me that he didn't want me to see them play until they were good enough for me. He told me that he was the lead guitarist and vocalist on some of their tracks.

Suddenly I realized that my boyfriend was really cool. And I wasn't. I had cheated on him. I was the bad guy. I decided at that moment that I had to do the right thing. I had to tell Finn the truth. Or most of it.

I told him about the party and how I'd set Sarah up.

"So let me get this straight: you were mad at Sarah because she beat you at a popularity contest you didn't care about, so you got her drunk and let some random guy pop her cherry?" He eyed me across the table.

I nodded.

"Damn, cheerleaders are mean."

I started to say, "I feel so much better having told you…" but he cut me off.

"You feel better? No, Bree. You're not going to feel better for a while. You're going to make it up to Sarah, and you're going to be punished."

"How am I supposed to make it up to Sarah?" I whined. It wasn't like her virginity was going to grow back just because I apologized.

"Figure it out. But your punishment starts right now. Come over here and pull up your skirt. You're way overdue for a spanking." He smiled happily; I could tell he was enjoying his chance to get back at me for what I'd done to him with a cucumber our first time

together. But I knew I needed to be punished.

Over the Knee

Finn sat back in his chair and I bent over his lap. He ordered me to pull up my skirt and I reached back obediently and pulled it up over my hips, exposing my firm cheeks in my white panties. He ordered me to pull my panties down, so I reached back and pulled them down to my knees.

Bent over his lap, my bare bottom in the air, right in his mom's kitchen, felt so dirty and wild and submissive. I knew I needed to be punished, but it was turning me on. I could feel his hand hovering in the air over my ass. The first spank landed, hard, and stung.

"Ow!" I yelped, squirming, but he held me down firmly with one hand while the other one turning my ass pink. Spank after spank landed, and not playful spanks. He was really giving me a spanking! For some reason, even though it hurt both my ass and my pride, I was suddenly so wet. And I could feel him getting hard under me. All that squirming will do that to a boy.

When Finn could tell from my plaintive yelps that I'd had enough, the spankings stopped and his hand rested on my bright red ass. I looked up at him over my shoulder. He was eyeing my ass hungrily.

"Can I fuck you in the ass?" he almost moaned.

"Are you asking me... or telling me?" I teased.

"I'm going to fuck you in the ass," he said, more confidently. "Get up. I'm going to fuck you in the ass!" My confident, strong boyfriend was taking control. I got up and let him lead me to his bedroom while I followed meekly. I wanted him to feel powerful. I lay face down on the bed while he unbuttoned his pants. I was so turned on I could hardly wait.

He put some lube on his cock and slowly, gently pushed his cock into my ass. I tried to relax, letting him in. It did hurt, but not as bad as I feared. It was more uncomfortable than painful. But even with the discomfort, the idea of Finn inside my ass after he'd spanked me was so hot that I was squirming with excitement. Finn's hand slid under me and found my clitoris, and he began to rhythmically rub my clit while he fucked my ass. My orgasm was almost immediate.

When we were done, he stroked my hair almost apologetically. "Did it hurt?" he asked, genuinely concerned.

I smiled up at him, "Did it hurt when I fucked you in the ass?"

He laughed, "Yeah, actually, it kinda did!" He kissed me softly. "Bree, so, maybe this means we're more fifty-fifty in this relationship now? Equals?"

"Hmmm... well, I'll give you sixty-forty. Final offer."

He kissed my neck and ears and cheeks. "Sixty-forty? I would have settled for seventy-thirty!"

But it did feel like our relationship was progressing into a more balanced dynamic. Instead of wanting to use him for my sexual needs, I wanted to serve his sexual needs. And he wanted to serve mine. Both of us serving each other in bed felt so romantic. I smiled whenever I thought about him.

"Now get up, get dressed, and go see Sarah," he ordered confidently and with a smile. I was dreading it, but I got into my car and drove to Sarah's house.

Making Amends

Sarah slapped me. Hard. I stood there and took it. My face stung. Two people had hit me in the last hour. I couldn't blame either of them.

We stood in Sarah's room and she trembled, tears forming. "But why, Bree?" she cried. "Why? I thought we were friends?"

I wanted to hug her but I didn't dare. She was like the little sister I'd always wanted, and I'd betrayed her. I told her I didn't know why I'd done it; I guessed I was just jealous about Homecoming and Jake and the Kittens.

"But I was just trying to be more like you!" she said through her tears. She looked so hurt.

I knew it was true. She was just like me. She was a real leader of the girls in the Kittens and was really effective. She was a great cheerleader and would obviously be cheer captain someday. And people liked her – no matter how much politicking you do, you aren't going to win Homecoming queen unless you're popular. It really hit me what an awful thing I'd done.

"I know," I said quietly, my own tears forming. I told her about losing my own virginity. I told her I formed the Kittens just to make money to impress an older man. I told her everything.

She wiped her tears and asked me lots of questions. We sat on her bed and talked. Finally we hugged. We agreed that no one would know what happened in Matt's bedroom that night. All the girls were so drunk and coked up that none of them had mentioned it. Maybe they didn't know. That meant only Sarah, me, Jake, and Finn knew. And we could manage them. And we agreed that we'd split the Kittens, fifty-fifty, and share all the decision-making and profits equally.

"So, are we good?" I looked at her hopefully.

"Not yet. There's one more thing," she said. She paused, looking me directly in the eyes. "I want you to go down on me."

"What?" I gasped.

"Yeah. You're going down on me, Bree, and you're going to do a very good job. And I'm going to take a picture. That way if you ever decide to go full-bitch on me again, I'll have that picture waiting."

I gave her a little kittenish smile and twirled my hair, "Oh, Sarah, you only had to ask!" She laughed. I figured giving her some power over me was only fair; I'd abused my power over her. Besides, I'd never even kissed a girl before – the idea got me so hot. And I was here on Finn's orders, so he couldn't get mad at me for it.

Soon she was lying back on her bed, her eyes closed, clenching the sheets while I buried my face between her young thighs. I gently licked and sucked her clitoris while my fingers massaged her g-spot inside her wet little pussy.

I felt so hot. I tasted her sweet young pussy, licking gently and harder, sucking gently and harder. I thought about Finn fucking me in the ass while my tongue worked Sarah's squirming body. I had her moaning and I felt her entire body tense before she released in a powerful orgasm.

Sarah gasped and moaned, "Oh Bree... that was amazing!"

I looked up, my face wet with her juices, and smiled. And then I froze with horror. Sarah's mom was standing at the door. She saw me between Sarah's legs on her bed. I jumped up.

Sarah yelled in outraged indignation and utter humiliation, "Mom! Get out!"

Her mom closed the door. We got dressed, barely able to meet each other's eyes. Downstairs at the kitchen table, her mother was waiting for us.

"Sarah, I want you to know that your father and I will love you no matter what," her mom started. Great. We were about to get a speech about her enlightened acceptance of our gayness.

"Later, mom," Sarah said firmly and we walked out.

Outside, Sarah said, "Fuck, Bree. You're like a one-girl demolition crew."

I nodded. "Yeah, that didn't exactly go according to plan."

"Yeah, that's why I'm going to help with the planning from now on. And you should know that my mom is probably calling your mom right now."

I smiled at Sarah and rolled my eyes and she smiled back. We shook our heads and laughed. Moms!

"Fuck," I said, "My face must have looked like a glazed donut from all your juices when I looked up at her from between your legs!"

"Yeah, great, she's going to want to talk all night long. I've now had sex twice: once with a guy I barely knew, and the second time with the girl who pimped me out to that guy."

I walked to my car and smiled back over my shoulder, "Oh, Sarah, you're so hot!" I yelled. "Let's do that again sometime!"

"Shut up!" she squealed, laughing. "My mom definitely heard that!"

A Well-Oiled Machine

Sarah made some changes to the Kittens; she decided how much each girl's tip was based on recommendations from the party cheer captain. The girls worked a lot harder knowing they'd be rewarded for their own effort, and anyone who slacked off or showed up late risked their tips.

She also added more girls, which allowed us to host more parties. She figured out that each party only needed one super-hot girl as a cheer captain, not five hot girls. We could build teams with four average-girls and one super-hot girl. It turned out that the average girls were much better workers with much less drama. They were even grateful for the job, rather than whining about how they'd miss a date with a boy or something. After a few months, Sarah changed it again so the cheer captain was the hardest-working girl and the hot girl – the eye candy

– worked for her. The hot girls, especially Lindsay and Kylie, were really lording it over the other girls and demanding bigger tips. Now they had their tips determined by the new hard-working cheer captain. Suddenly the hot girls got a lot sweeter.

Sarah even hired a heavyset girl with bad skin named Erica as our 'office manager', even though we had no office. She managed bookings, maintained the website, and handle any last-minute scheduling problems. And Erica was the coolest girl. She always brought me coffee or a little treat whenever we were working late, and she arranged for boys to do my homework. I liked her a lot more than the popular girls.

And Sarah and Erica insisted that all our parties be mainstream and legitimate. No more pimping out girls. Without a need for those kinds of parties, I lost touch with Matt. I didn't miss him. I'm sure he found another girl to bounce off his bed. And I kinda felt sorry for him: I'm sure he got laid a lot, but how could he ever find love? And sex with Finn was better than ever now that we were in love with each other.

With their management, our bookings went up and tips went through the roof. With Erica managing things, Sarah and I started building teams at other local high schools. One weekend we had ten parties on the same Saturday. At $500 a party, that was a $5,000 in a single night. We paid out $2,500 to the girls and split $2,500 between the two of us. We were rolling in cash. Our wardrobes were growing and I couldn't stop looking a two-year-old black BMW three-series that was on sale nearby.

The Football Party

After school one day, Erica pulled Sarah and me aside. "We got an interesting booking," Ericas said. She explained that we'd received an online booking request for us to host an end-of-season party for a football team. Our school's rival football team. Sarah and I instantly shook our heads no. Our football team had destroyed their team. It wasn't close. It was obvious they wanted to get their revenge on our cheerleaders.

But Erica said that she'd rejected the request but had gotten a call immediately. The kid calling said that, yeah, they wanted to have their rivals' cheerleaders cheer for them at their party, but they would be perfectly respectful and they'd host the party at a nearby country club with lots of adult supervision. And they'd pay double.

"And there's one other thing," Erica continued, "He was adamant that Sarah attend."

Sarah looked at me. "Do I have 'rape me' written on my ass or something?"

We talked it over; it was intriguing, but too dangerous. Our school rivals were on the richer side of town; the girls were a little excited to work a party in a real country club. A lot of the girls were bored working parties for their parents. And it was more than a little hot that the football team wanted us badly enough to pay double.

I called the boy back myself. He actually sounded nice. He told me they were handing out awards and all the graduating seniors would get recognized. He wanted us to cheer for them; he thought it would be fun because their seniors had never beaten our team in their high school football careers. All their parents would be there. That sounded pretty safe; they couldn't exactly gang-rape us in front of their moms, could they? I reluctantly agreed to do it on the condition that there would be no social media allowed. I wasn't going to let them post pictures of our cheerleaders with their football players.

He agreed, but before he hung up, he asked again, "So, that girl Sarah, she'll be there, right?"

"Why?" I asked.

"Oh, it's just, well, you know, a lot of guys want her to be there, for, because..." he stammered, suddenly tongue-tied.

"I need a good reason, or she's not going," I said. We didn't need the business badly enough to set up Sarah for another fucking by some guy who didn't care about her. She still hadn't slept with Jake; I wasn't putting her in another bad situation.

"I just think she's... beautiful," he said.

"Fine," I said. I could tell by his voice that he meant it. I hung up.

We all drove over to the country club together. It was immaculate, with manicured lawns and landscaped gardens surrounding a cool white building. It looked so civilized, so serene. Men in the parking lot with expensive cars stopped pulling golf bags out of their trunks to watch a parade of hot young cheerleaders in uniform walk to the front doors of the country club.

I walked bravely into the conference room leading my cheerleaders like little ducklings in a line behind me; I could hear boys' voices and knew it was our room. The room had expensive carpets and comfortable chairs; the tables were set with white tablecloths. A tall good-looking sandy-haired boy

walked nervously up to me. "Are you Bree?" I
nodded.

He introduced himself as Adam. He was their
quarterback; the one I'd spoken to on the phone.
While we talked, he looked over my shoulder at the
girls walking in behind me. It was obvious he was
looking for Sarah. When his eyes found her, he
suddenly stammered nervously and told me we could
just hang out until the award ceremony when we'd
cheer. Then, instead of approaching Sarah like I
thought he would, he retreated back with his friends.

I saw the way he looked at Sarah throughout the
party. The party was pretty boring; we just stood
there while the boys nervously checked us out. They
warmed up a little when their coach started handing
out awards. But the quarterback slumped nervously
in his chair, his eyes always returning to Sarah. I
remembered that he'd been checking Sarah out

during the Homecoming game. Suddenly I realized that this party wasn't about revenge; this boy was in love with Sarah!

We performed our cheers for the boys as they got their awards. With their parents and coaches there, the boys kept their comments pretty mild, but I could tell they liked the show. We didn't wear the slutty uniforms we wore to Homecoming but our regular uniforms were revealing enough. After the awards were handed out and everyone ate cake, some of the boys gathered their courage to talk to my girls.

But not their quarterback, Adam. He stayed in the corner, talking to his friends, his coaches, his parents. But his eyes drifted across the room, constantly looking for Sarah. It was cute. But I could tell he needed my help. I found Sarah.

"Sarah, I want to introduce you to someone." I led her over to Adam. "Adam, have you met Sarah? Sarah, Adam is the one who booked the party."

Sarah smiled at him. She was oblivious to his desire. She smiled up at him and said, "We were pretty nervous when we got the booking! I thought you guys hated us!"

Adam smiled back nervously. "Hate you? No... well, I mean, we don't like your football team that much, but I couldn't hate you." He blushed.

Sarah kept chatting with him. How could she be this oblivious? It was so obvious that Adam was into her. I could see his teammates nudging each other; they all obviously knew that Adam liked Sarah, too. I left them to talk.

Another boy, a giant black football player with a huge head, came up to me and whispered, "Nice move. He's been talking about her since the game but doesn't have the balls to make a move." He explained that he was the one who found our website and told Adam to book us for the party; he was sick of hearing Adam mooning over Sarah. He'd even convinced some of the players' fathers to pay for our services.

The boy, Ty, told me that Adam was a really good guy. He'd won a scholarship to play college football next year but wasn't just some arrogant quarterback. "He's easily the nicest kid in our school." I looked up at the boy towering over me and told him, "Sarah's pretty nice, too." We looked over at them. It was painfully obvious even from across the room that Adam was hopelessly in love with Sarah. And that Sarah liked him back. Ty smiled, "Cute couple."

As we left, I saw Sarah take a Sharpie and write her number in permanent ink on Adam's powerful forearm. Ty smiled and gave me a nudge on the shoulder, but with his giant-sized arms, even a little nudge hurt. "Ow!" I said and punched him back. I don't think he felt it.

But I gave Ty a smile as I left and said, "Nice of you to look out for your quarterback like that."

He just shrugged and said, "I'm his left tackle."

I knew from years of cheerleading that the left tackle is responsible for protecting the quarterback. Hooking him up with Sarah may or may not turn out to be protecting Adam, but it was nice anyway.

I thought of Jake as we drove away. That guy was never getting laid.

Feminist Warrior

Erica helped me with my college applications. I'd started writing them with a focus on my cheer captaincy and student council leadership. Erica ripped it all up.

She told me, "Every American high school has a bunch of empty-headed cheer Nazis, Bree. But how many schools have a feminist icon?"

Erica reinvented me as a feminist: a wildly successful young entrepreneur who hired only women and a student leader who created an empowerment study hall to improve the self-esteem of the girls who were most vulnerable. She conveniently left out the parts about me riding cocks like a rodeo bull rider or pimping out my fellow students.

"Once you're on campus, you might want to hide out, though: when they see you're not a frumpy unshaven granola-eating man-hater, they'll kick you out of the feminist club."

Our school counselor reviewed my applications while Erica and Sarah sat in her office chewing their nails and I sat on the edge of her desk painting mine. The counselor nodded through all of it and sighed happily at the end.

"Bree, I can't tell you how proud I am of you," she said, standing and wrapping me in a hug. I smelled like lilacs for the rest of the day.

Outside her office, I told Erica and Sarah that I owed them one. Erica sighed, "Get me laid then."

Just One More Scheme

Sarah and I hatched a plan. Jake had been adrift since Sarah left him for Adam; his whole world had crumbled around him in a few short months. He'd started the year dating me, the cheer captain, and then switched to Sarah, the new Homecoming queen; he was the king of the locker room and the envy of every boy. But he hadn't nailed either of us, and now he was alone.

Sarah and I enlisted help from all our friends; we were going to do to Jake what had been done to Sarah and me. We were going to get him drunk and laid. There was a party that Friday night; a boy's parents were out of town and he was having a blowout. We told Finn and Adam that we were going out without them because we had plans with our ex-boyfriend; they shrugged and made plans together.

"Thank God, a night with no business talk," Finn said.

"Yeah, we should go pick up chicks," Adam added. "Maybe some dumb cheerleaders who just want to talk about movies and makeup."

Sarah rolled her eyes. I just laughed and said, "Yeah, right. I guarantee you two will be texting us before midnight telling us how much you miss us."

It was hard to get Jake to the party. He was so mopey these days. But some of his friends on his cross-country team talked him into it for us. Sarah and I didn't want to tip him off by inviting him directly. But at the party, we made sure he found us at the makeshift bar in the basement. We acted a little drunk and insisted he drink some shots with us. We drank water; we fed him vodka.

Erica was a little on the heavy side and her skin wasn't great, but Sarah had taken her to the spa. Her hair was curled and her makeup was flawless. She wore a very flattering skirt, but the top was my pick: she had enormous breasts. I made sure they were pouring out of her top.

Once Jake was a little drunk, Erica came up to the bar with us. Sarah and I had her join us; I saw Jake's eyes find her ample breasts. Erica was a little drunk and giggly, and she leaned over the bar, making sure her breasts were on full display, and flirted with Jake. And Jake, quiet at first, flirted back. Sarah and I drifted away, leaving them alone.

It wasn't long before I saw Erica leading Jake by his hand into a quiet bedroom. Sarah guarded the door like a she-lion; she wasn't letting anyone interrupt Erica.

Sarah, Erica, and I became inseparable, walking the halls of our high school like lionesses patrolling our territory. Whenever anyone snickered about the fat girl and the two cheerleaders, Sarah and I used our powers for evil. Finn would just shake his head and mumble something about demonic cheerleaders whenever he saw how we'd attack. We'd have girls in tears almost instantly by posting a little mean-spirited comment online about her stringy hair or ugly shoes. But a kitten's got to keep her claws sharp, right?

It's Pink!

A few months later, I finally got to hear Finn's band. They played at a dank basement coffee shop near the college campus. I asked Sarah and Adam to double-date so I'd have someone to sit with, but Sarah had told everyone so by the time we got there we had about fifteen people with us.

We did not belong in there. Grungy college kids, metal poseurs, and the rest of a bunch of the perpetually-gloomy eyed us as we walked in. Kylie was wearing a short pink dress in the hopes of meeting a boy, Adam had on a white polo. Jake and Erica were holding hands but looked a little nervous.

Everyone else in the place was wearing black.

Finn's band played and it was all I could do to keep from covering my ears in pain. God, did they suck. They played some horrible post-metal bass-heavy droning mess. The girl bassist posed self-

consciously and played the same note over and over.

Her two friends sat in the front dressed all in black

and chair-danced like morons. The drummer must

have been seriously high because he just hammered

the drums like a madman. He couldn't possibly be

playing the same song as the rest of the band.

But Finn's guitar playing turned me on. That night

my parents were out of town and I took my guitar-

playing boyfriend home with me.

Other than picking me up for Homecoming, Finn

hadn't been in my house. We sat in the kitchen and

talked about his band and my business. He

strummed on his guitar while I painted my toenails

pink. I felt so comfortable with him.

When my nails dried I stood up, wiggled my toes, and smiled, "Aren't you rock stars supposed to nail your groupies?"

He smiled happily as I led him up into my pink bedroom.

"You know how you want me to be more feminine in the bedroom?" I smiled at Finn and sat on my bed. He looked at me apprehensively. I pulled out some handcuffs and a giant pink dildo from under my pillow. His eyes grew wide when he saw the dildo.

"It's pink, Finn! It's so feminine! Come on, baby, let me fuck you with it!" I giggled.

"Oh, hell, no," he said as he backed away.

I chased him around the house with the giant pink dildo. "Don't play hard to get, kitten!" I laughed, waving it in the air. I loved that guy.

Postscript

I followed the directions Erica had given me and drove up the driveway past a manicured lawn to a huge house that backed up to the 9th hole of a private golf course next to the same country club we'd been to for Adam's football party. Sarah had warned me to be careful, but I wasn't worried. I opened the door without ringing the bell and walked right into the house. There were photos of a family on the walls; a man and his wife and three kids. I went straight to the living room. I saw five or six Nordstrom bags by the couch. He had taken them shopping.

He was sitting on the couch quietly sipping on a glass of bourbon, his feet up on the coffee table. On the floor were Lindsay and Kylie, both wearing nothing but diapers. They were playing with dolls. The man had his pants around his knees and his cock in his hand. He was masturbating while he watched the girls.

I sat down next to him on the couch while he furiously tugged on his cock. I checked a couple text messages and then looked over at him. Our eyes met briefly then he went back to concentrating on the girls.

"Roger, we need to talk," I sighed.

He ignored me. "Kylie, I think you made pee-pee in your diaper, you bad girl." Kylie looked up, her eyes glazed, and smiled at me. Obviously Roger was giving the girls lots of recreational drugs. "Oh, hi, Bree," she smiled. "I need a diaper change!" she giggled.

I rolled my eyes. Kylie lay back on the rug. "Daddy, will you change me?" she smiled up at him. Roger nodded and baby-talked, "Of course I'll change my

Roger returned to the couch and immediately had his cock back in his hand. I whispered to him, "Finish up, Roger, and meet me in the kitchen."

Roger had a guilty smile on his face when he entered the kitchen. I sat on the counter, slowly swinging my long legs and dangling my sandals from my feet. Roger's eyes found my feet immediately.

"Where's the wife, Roger?"

He didn't look up. "Took the kids to the beach for the weekend." But he knew I'd caught him and he knew he was in trouble. "It's just some harmless fun!" he whined. "I never touch them!"

"Roger, if you want to see my girls, you talk to me first. And you pay me. You've been very bad. How would you like me to take baby Lindsay and baby Kylie away forever?"

Roger looked at me, fear in his eyes. He was obviously addicted to them. "Bree, I just needed to see them. I bought them a lot of stuff, I was going to tell you..."

"Roger, I see it this way: you owe me for the time with my girls. And you owe me a penalty for taking them without my permission. And now you have to pre-pay me for any time you want with them in the future."

Roger sighed. He couldn't say no.

"How many times have you seen them?"

He looked up sheepishly. "Three."

"Here's what we're going to do, " I said. "You're going to pay me $1,000 for each time you've seen them. That's $3,000. Then you're going to pay me a 100% penalty for breaking the rules. That's another $3,000. So that's $6,000." I thought about it for a second and added, "Each."

He looked up, shocked. "$12,000? I can't do that!" he protested.

I sighed. "You can, and you will. You can drop it off in cash at cheer practice on Monday. We'll be on the outdoor field. And Roger, from now on you'll pay me in advance, understand?"

Roger understood me completely. I knew where he lived and where he worked. If he didn't keep me happy, his whole world would come crumbling down. But he wasn't willing – or wasn't able – to give up his sexual desires. I owned him.

From the Author

The Kittens is my debut novel. You can connect with me at allisonangel.wordpress.com or on the usual social media. If you enjoyed the novel, please take the time to write a review. It really helps!

Thanks,

Allison

www.ingramcontent.com/pod-product-compliance
Lightning Source LLC
Chambersburg PA
CBHW051235260626
47162CB00002B/437